PRAISE FOR A

'I absolutely adore this series and this one was my favourite so far. A gripping plot and plenty of charm. Thank you!'

— AMAZON FIVE STAR REVIEW

'She's done it again. Another beautifully crafted and compelling pony mystery with real, relatable characters.'

— AMAZON FIVE STAR REVIEW

'This book is sure to be a winner with all pony lovers.'

— AMAZON FIVE STAR REVIEW

THE HUNT FOR THE GOLDEN HORSE

AMANDA WILLS

P oppy McKeever woke with a start, her heart hammering. The nightmare was so vivid she could feel the roughness of the blanket that covered her mum's face and taste the seawater saltiness of unshed tears at the back of her throat. She sat up and drew her knees tightly to her chest. Magpie, curled in a ball at the foot of the bed, lifted his head and watched her with unblinking green eyes.

It was years since she'd dreamed about the accident. In the ten years since it happened time had blurred the edges of her grief. These days, if she ever forced herself to replay the events of that awful afternoon, it was as though she was watching a grainy black and white film, with actors playing the roles. It felt remote, detached from her. But the dream had thrown everything into three dimensional horror.

Poppy could see the wide eyes of the driver as he wrenched the steering wheel to the right, a second too late. She could feel the air being squeezed out of her lungs as Hannah's mum clutched her to her chest, shielding her from the sight of the ambulance as it drove off in silence. Poppy hadn't understood why the sirens had been switched off. It wasn't until much later that she realised why.

She hugged her knees, wondering what trick of her subconscious had made her relive that terrible afternoon. She checked the time on her mobile. Half-past four. Soon the sky would turn pink and the dawn chorus would begin, the start of another glorious late spring day on Dartmoor. But now her bedroom was still cocooned in velvety darkness. Poppy reached for Magpie. At the touch of her hand the old cat stood up, stretched, and lumbered up the bed, settling beside her. Poppy coiled herself around his warm bulk and steadied her breathing until her pulse stopped racing and her eyelids grew heavy. Sleep, when it finally returned, was deep and dreamless.

'ARE YOU OK?' Caroline asked, as Poppy sat slumped at the kitchen table, nibbling unenthusiastically on a corner of toast.

'Didn't sleep very well.'

Her stepmum smiled indulgently. 'Excited about the holidays, I expect.'

Poppy pushed her plate away and stood up. 'Something like that.' She gave Caroline a quick smile. It wasn't her fault, after all. 'Better go and feed the neddies before they call out a search party.' Plucking the biggest carrot from the vegetable rack, Poppy headed for the back door just as the phone started ringing.

Cloud, Chester and Jenny were at the far side of the field, grazing side by side under the leafy green canopy of a vast oak tree. It was funny, thought Poppy. When she'd brought Jenny home she'd been worried that her arrival might cause friction between Cloud and Chester. Two's company and all that. Far from it. They rubbed along together just fine.

Cloud saw her and whinnied, his brown eyes fixed on hers as she tramped across the field. She ruffled his forelock and he nibbled the pocket of her shorts in search of the carrot.

'That's to share,' she scolded him gently, snapping it in three. Cloud and Chester crunched theirs noisily and wandered off. Jenny waited patiently for her turn, her lips as soft as a kiss as she snuffled the carrot from Poppy's palm.

Poppy ran her hand through the donkey's seal-grey coat. She was plump and content, unrecognisable as the skinny creature George Blackstone had dragged along to the donkey auditions the previous Christmas. Five months of five star care had seen to that.

The donkey's long ears snapped forward and she gave a low heehaw. Poppy was surprised to see Charlie sprinting across the field towards them, his face flushed.

'Guess what?' he panted, skidding to a halt in front of them.

'The real Charlie was kidnapped by aliens in the night and you are in fact an evil imposter?'

Charlie shook his head impatiently. 'You know your friend Hannah from Twickenham?'

'Of course I do. Why?'

'Her mum just rang. She's coming to stay!'

'Sarah's coming to stay?' said Poppy, bemused.

'No! *Hannah's* coming to stay. Her mum's got to have an operation and her dad's away on business. She's just asked Mum if Hannah can stay with us for half-term and Mum's said yes. She's arriving tomorrow morning!'

Poppy rested her hand on Jenny's wither. 'Cool.'

'You don't sound very excited,' said Charlie.

She gave a little shake of her head. 'Of course I am. It's just been a long time, that's all.'

Three years in fact. She'd kept in touch with Hannah by email when they'd first moved to Riverdale, but as the months passed the emails had grown fewer and farther in between, eventually drying up altogether. Poppy couldn't remember the last time she'd heard from Hannah. They'd been eleven when they last saw each other. Poppy had been mad about ponies. Hannah had wanted to be a famous pop star. Poppy read voraciously. Hannah was more interested in clothes and listening to music. Poppy was an introvert. Hannah was the total opposite, and yet their friendship had always worked. They'd known each other since pre-school and their mums had been close friends. They'd been inseparable until the McKeevers' move to Devon three years before.

Now they were fourteen. Poppy was still mad about ponies, although she wasn't as shy as she'd once been. Did Hannah still want to win X Factor? Poppy had no idea. Would they still get on? Poppy wasn't even sure she'd recognise Hannah if she passed her in the street.

As she followed Charlie back to the house, she mulled over the news. She hadn't thought about her old best friend for months and months, and in less than twenty four hours she would be here. Poppy couldn't decide if she was excited or terrified.

Scarlett stared at Poppy, frown lines crinkling her forehead. 'Hannah's coming to stay? Here? At Riverdale?'

'I know. Crazy, isn't it? I haven't seen her for years.'

'For the whole half-term?' The crinkles became deep furrows.

Poppy shrugged her shoulders apologetically. 'Her mum's having an operation. I don't think Caroline felt she had much choice.'

Scarlett disappeared into Red's stable. When she finally spoke, her voice was muffled. 'What about all our plans? The picnic on the moor, the cross country clinic? She's not going to want to do any of that, is she? You said all she's interested in is boys, make-up and music. She's not going to want to spend all day with the ponies, is she?'

Poppy fiddled with a hank of Cloud's mane. 'I know, but what can I do? Perhaps she can stay at home with Caroline and Charlie when we go off and do all those things.'

Scarlett made a noise that was halfway between a harrumph and a tsk. Poppy peered into the stable. Her best friend was staring at the floor, her mouth turned down at the corners. She didn't even smile when Red picked up his bucket in his mouth and dropped it at her feet.

'I'm sorry, Scar. But it'll be fine. We can all hang out together. It'll be fun,' Poppy said.

Scarlett sighed loudly and led the chestnut gelding out of the stable. 'If you say so.'

THEY RODE in silence for the first half an hour as they skirted the Riverdale tor and headed towards the old quarry where Cloud had found Poppy the day she and Charlie were lost on the moor. The sky was a swirly mass of grey clouds that threatened rain. How appropriate, thought Poppy, glancing at Scarlett's thunderous expression. She decided to tease her friend out of her black mood.

'Well, this is nice,' she joked. 'A lovely hack on the moor with beautiful views and scintillating conversation.'

Scarlett looked a little shamefaced. 'Sorry. It's just that I had been looking forward to the holiday so much. It's been such a busy term.'

She was right. Their teachers had really cranked up the pace since Christmas and they had two weeks of exams ahead of them when they went back to school.

'If it makes you feel any better I'm not sure I want Hannah to come and stay, either.'

Scarlett looked surprised. 'But you've been best buddies with her way longer than we've been friends.'

'I know. But I haven't seen her since I was eleven. People change.'

'What's she like?'

'Um, well, she's small and slim and has long, blonde hair.'

'I hate her already,' said Scarlett.

Poppy glanced over, her eyebrows raised.

Scarlett held up her hands. 'Only joking. Carry on.'

'She's not shy like me. She never used to be, anyway. She was an extrovert. A bit like you, come to think of it.' Was it inevitable that shy people sought out extroverts because they knew they'd coax them out of their shells, Poppy wondered.

'Does she like the countryside?'

'Of course,' Poppy said, although she couldn't really remember. 'And her favourite thing in the whole world is millionaire's shortbread. Same as you.'

'At least we have one thing in common.'

'Exactly,' Poppy agreed, glad that Scarlett finally seemed to be coming round to the idea that she and Hannah might actually be friends. 'I was thinking that if she wants to come out with us she can take my bike. It needn't stop all our plans.'

Scarlett cackled and kicked Red into a canter. 'That's if she can keep up with us,' she shouted over her shoulder as Red's long legs covered the ground in easy strides.

Poppy sighed as Cloud surged forward, keen not to be left behind. She had a horrible feeling there could be fireworks ahead.

3

Poppy surveyed the yard with narrowed eyes. It was
tidy, no-one could argue with that. She'd spent the
last two hours sweeping the concrete and wrestling
with the muck heap, cajoling the chaotic, creeping mess of
muck and straw into an orderly stack with towering sides
and regimented right-angles. The hose was neatly looped
over the outside tap and Poppy had used a rusty scythe she'd
found in the bike shed to cut swathes through the ferocious
wall of nettles between the muck heap and tack room.

It wasn't perfect by any stretch of the imagination. The
concrete was as pitted as the stone of a peach and there was a
dark stain outside Chester and Jenny's stable where she'd
accidentally tipped over a tub of creosote the previous
summer. The paint on the stable doors was peeling and
Chester had nibbled the red geraniums she'd planted in
terracotta pots either side of the tack room. But there was
nothing she could do about that now. Hannah would have to
take them as she found them.

Cloud watched her from his stable, his grey ears pricked.
Poppy's heart swelled with love. The stables may not be

perfect, but he was. She crossed the yard in a couple of steps and scratched his poll.

'Why am I so nervous?' she asked him.

He blew warm air into her neck, making her giggle. 'I know, it's silly, isn't it? It's only Hannah, after all.'

'THEY'RE HERE!' yelled Charlie from his vantage point on the landing.

Poppy, who had been rearranging the items on her dressing table for the hundredth time, dropped her hairbrush with a clatter and joined him. They watched as a metallic-grey BMW crunched up the Riverdale drive. Sarah was the first to emerge. Poppy took one look at her familiar face and was transported back to the day her mum died.

'She looks exactly the same,' she muttered with relief.

'Crikey, Hannah doesn't,' said Charlie, as they watched a tall girl with a choppy blonde bob uncurl herself gracefully from the passenger side and slam the door shut. Shielding her eyes from the sun, the girl stared up at the house. Poppy shrank behind the curtains, not wanting to be caught spying like some gauche kid. Charlie had no such compunction, and to Poppy's horror he threw the window open and started waving frantically. 'Hannah! *Hannah*! We're here!'

Hannah looked up, an unreadable expression on her face. Poppy realised her stomach was churning.

Charlie was already halfway along the landing. 'Come *on* Poppy!' he shouted.

She followed him down the stairs and out of the front door.

'Hi,' she said to the visitors, suddenly shy.

'Poppy!' Sarah cried. 'Look at you, all grown up!' She

studied Poppy's face. 'Beautiful,' she murmured. 'Just like your mum.'

Poppy swallowed the lump that had suddenly appeared in her throat. Sarah nodded, as if she understood, and hugged her tightly.

Hannah stepped forward. She was wearing a fitted navy teeshirt, denim miniskirt and navy Converse sneakers. Leather bracelets entwined each wrist and a dusky pink cardigan was tied casually around her waist. She looked city slick. Poppy stared glumly at her own faded red polo shirt, old navy jodhpurs and sock-clad feet.

'Alright?' said Hannah, her face straight.

Dismayed at the lukewarm greeting, Poppy cleared her throat. 'Yeah. Good. You?'

Hannah's mouth twitched at one corner and she held out her right fist. Poppy did the same. For a moment she was worried she had forgotten. But as Hannah tapped the top of her fist lightly it was instinctive. Tap, tap, fist bump and high five, ending with jazz fingers. They burst out laughing.

'You remembered!'

'As if I'd forget,' said Hannah. She gazed at the old stone cottage and the soft green mass of the Riverdale tor behind it. 'So, where's the nearest clothes shop?'

Poppy's heart sank. If Hannah was still obsessed with fashion, music and boys it was going to be a long week.

'Barney sells thermal socks in the village shop,' Charlie offered.

'I'm only kidding, Charlie-boy. It's nice to leave the big smoke behind.' Hannah linked arms with Poppy. 'So are you going to show me around or what?'

'Of course. What do you want to see first, my bedroom or the stables?'

'The stables, obvs! I've heard so much about Cloud and Chester. I can't wait to meet them.'

'I thought you weren't very interested in horses,' Poppy admitted, as they crossed the field to say hello to Cloud and the two donkeys.

'Ha! That's where you're wrong. I wasn't, I know. But I started having riding lessons last summer.'

'In Twickenham?' Poppy said, surprised.

'There's a riding school in Teddington. It even has its own Pony Club.'

Hannah tore handfuls of grass and offered them to Cloud, Chester and Jenny.

'You never told me!' said Poppy.

'I know. I've been rubbish at keeping in touch, haven't I? I ride a bay mare called Lady. She's about the same size as Cloud.'

The Connemara rubbed against Hannah, leaving a layer of white hairs on her navy top. She laughed as she brushed them off.

'He's gorgeous, Poppy.'

'I think so,' Poppy grinned. 'You can have a ride on him later, if you like. I'll see if Scarlett wants to come over.'

'She's your next door neighbour?'

'She's my best friend,' said Poppy without thinking. She felt a blush creep up her neck and shrugged helplessly. 'Sorry.'

'It's OK. I have a new best friend, too. Do you remember Cassie from primary school?'

Poppy had a vague memory of a curly-haired girl who had been captain of all the school sports teams. 'I think so.'

'We ended up in the same form at high school. She's the one who got me riding. I would have stayed with Cassie while Mum's in hospital, only she's in Florida for half-term.'

'Well, I'm glad you came here,' said Poppy with conviction. 'I think we're going to have a lot of fun.'

4

Her conviction wavered later that afternoon when Scarlett arrived. Hannah had already made herself at home, scattering her clothes, toiletries and books around Poppy's bedroom as if it was her own. She was sitting crosslegged on the wicker chair Scarlett usually occupied, chatting nineteen to the dozen, when there was a faint knock on the door.

Poppy jumped to her feet and pulled it open. 'Scarlett! Why are you knocking, you twit?'

Scarlett shrugged. 'Didn't want to interrupt you.' She smiled briefly at Hannah. 'Hiya.'

Hannah beckoned her in. 'I feel like I know you already, Scarlett O'Hara. Poppy's been telling me about all the adventures you've been having. You two really ought to write a book!'

'My surname's Spencer, not O'Hara.'

Hannah chortled. 'It was a joke, you know, like Scarlett O'Hara in Gone with the Wind?'

Scarlett rolled her eyes.

Poppy patted the bed beside her. 'Come and sit down,

Scar. We were just reminiscing about the old days. Then Hannah's going to have a ride on Cloud.'

'I thought you said she didn't like horses,' said Scarlett, perching on the edge of the bed.

'Hey, I am in the room you know,' said Hannah.

Scarlett flushed. 'Sorry. But Poppy said all you were interested in was clothes and music.'

Thanks Scarlett, Poppy groaned to herself. Hannah bristled.

'Clothes, music *and* horses, actually. I ride at a stables in London,' she said grandly. 'I specialise in dressage.'

'Poppy and I prefer jumping, don't we, Poppy?'

'Umm,' said Poppy, her head swivelling between her two friends. This was not going to plan at all. She slid off the bed. 'I'll go and see if those brownies are ready. Won't be a sec.'

Caroline was sitting at the kitchen table, staring blankly into the middle distance, The Daily Telegraph open in front of her.

'What's up?' said Poppy.

She gave a little shake of her head. 'I can't believe it. Cormac O'Sullivan has died.'

'Cormac O'Who?' Poppy made a beeline for the brownies, which were cooling on a wire rack by the toaster.

'Only the lead singer of Cormac and the Sullivans. My favourite all-time band when I was a bit older than you.'

'Never heard of them.'

Caroline smiled down at the paper. Poppy glanced over her shoulder. A man in black leather trousers and a ripped black teeshirt stared back at her with a challenge in his eyes. He looked edgy and cool.

'They were an indie rock band. I went to see them at the Hammersmith Odeon once. Best night of my life,' said Caroline wistfully.

'Does Dad know?' grinned Poppy.

Caroline laughed. 'No. It was just a schoolgirl crush. But Cormac was a proper old school rock star, you know? Lived in a mansion, spent his fortune on partying and fast cars. Oh, and horses. He loved horses. The band did a cover of Wild Horses by the Rolling Stones. It was number one for weeks.'

Poppy patted her shoulder. 'Before my time, I'm afraid.'

'Don't make me feel any more ancient than I do already.' Caroline folded the paper. 'Poor Cormac. Anyway, how's it going up there?'

Poppy groaned. 'Not good. Hannah and Scarlett don't seem to have hit it off. At all.'

'Oh dear.'

'I thought that because I like them both, and they both like me, they would automatically like each other. Apparently not.' Poppy took a brownie and rammed it into her mouth. 'Mmm, these are yummy.'

'I threw some pecans into the mixture,' said Caroline, piling half a dozen brownies onto a plate, which she handed to Poppy. 'Take some up. They might help.'

'As long as they don't start throwing them at each other,' said Poppy gloomily. 'Wish me luck.'

Hannah was scrolling through photos on her mobile phone and Scarlett was leafing through the latest copy of Poppy's pony magazine when she returned. The silence was deafening.

Scarlett took two brownies but when Poppy offered them to Hannah she patted her stomach, glanced at Scarlett and shook her head. 'No thanks. I'm watching my weight.'

Poppy chewed in silence as Hannah recounted anecdote after anecdote from their primary school days.

'Do you remember that time in Year Four when we went to the Natural History Museum and got lost in the dinosaur exhibition? They had to put out a tannoy message telling us to meet Mrs Finch by the Tyrannosaurus?' Hannah laughed at the memory. 'She looked more ferocious than the T-Rex by the time we arrived. She was incandescent, wasn't she? And what about that time I made you do a dance routine for the talent show, only you got stage fright and I had to dance around you and pretend it was all part of the act.' Hannah looked at Scarlett kindly. 'You had to be there.'

Scarlett scowled into the pages of the magazine. Poppy fidgeted on the bed. The walls of her room seemed to be closing in on the three of them. Perhaps if they were out in the fresh air they might not be so scratchy with each other.

'Come on, you two,' she said, hauling herself to her feet like an old woman. 'Let's go and find Cloud.'

5

Scarlett hung on the five bar gate watching Poppy as she tightened Cloud's girth, ran down his stirrups and gave Hannah a leg-up.

Poppy stood back, her hands on her hips. 'How does he feel?'

Hannah gathered her reins and flashed her a smile. 'Great.'

'Just remember he's not a riding school pony. He might be a bit sharper than Lady.'

Hannah was about to retort when a magpie swooped onto the ground in front of them. Cloud skittered sideways. Hannah yelped, let go of the reins and grabbed a handful of his mane. Poppy's hand shot out automatically to grasp his bridle.

'Steady boy,' she murmured, scratching his poll until he stood quietly. She looked up at Hannah. Her face was pale.

'See what I mean?'

'I was fine. It made me jump, that's all.'

'OK,' said Poppy mildly. 'Do you want to have a walk and trot in a circle? The ground's a bit hard in here for cantering.'

After a wet spring and a dry few days the ground was actually beautifully soft and springy, perfect for a canter, but Poppy thought she'd better get an idea of Hannah's competency before they tried anything faster than a trot. Cloud was known to throw in an occasional buck when he was feeling particularly bouncy, and the last thing Poppy wanted was for her friend to fall off.

Satisfied Cloud had settled, she gave him a brisk pat and went to join Scarlett by the gate. Hannah tightened her reins and booted Cloud in the ribs. He grunted, flicked his ears back and launched into a fast walk. They completed a rather jagged circle and she kicked him into a trot.

'She's not very good, is she?' said Scarlett with satisfaction. 'She's not even on the right diagonal.'

'Scarlett!' chided Poppy. 'She's only been riding since last summer. I probably didn't know my left diagonal from my right when I first started, either.'

'You did. I taught you them, remember.'

Hannah slowed Cloud to a walk and changed reins.

'Look how stiff she is. She's not moving with him,' said Scarlett.

Poppy realised her best friend was right. Hannah certainly sat straight in the saddle and her feet and hands were in the right position, but she looked tense. She was also holding the reins too tightly and Cloud, clearly uncomfortable, kept giving little shakes of his head.

'Try loosening your reins a little. He doesn't like a really tight rein,' Poppy called. Hannah let the reins slip through her fingers until they were flapping like washing lines. 'Not too much, though. You just need to keep a light contact with his mouth.'

It felt weird seeing someone else ride her pony. Charlie had ridden Cloud on the lead rein a couple of times, but no-one else had, not even Scarlett. A strange emotion squeezed Poppy's insides. She had a horrible feeling it was jealousy.

Cloud napped as he passed the gate to the stables and Hannah almost lost her seat.

'She really is useless,' said Scarlett.

'You know what she needs?' said Poppy decisively.

'I can think of a few things.'

'I'll pretend I didn't hear that. What she needs is a decent teacher.'

'Who were you thinking, Bella?'

'No. I was thinking of you actually. You taught me so well, after all. Everything kind of made sense when you explained it to me.' Poppy looked sidelong at Scarlett, hoping she hadn't overdone the flattery. But Scarlett was smiling modestly.

'People do say I have a natural talent for instruction,' she agreed. 'Well, Mum says I'm a terrible bossy boots, anyway.'

They both giggled.

'I think Cloud is probably a bit too fizzy for her, too,' said Poppy. 'I don't suppose you'd let her ride Flynn?'

Flynn was the solid and dependable Dartmoor pony Scarlett had taught Poppy to ride on. He belonged to Alex, Scarlett's older brother, but Alex was a shade under six foot and hadn't ridden him for years.

'He could certainly do with the exercise,' Scarlett admitted.

'Go on, Scar. Think how much fun it'll be to lord it over Hannah.'

Scarlett chewed her thumbnail.

'I'll poo pick and muck out for you while you give her lessons.'

'And scrub the water trough?'

Poppy sighed. 'Alright.'

Scarlett grinned evilly. 'I think a lot of sitting trot without stirrups is what she needs, don't you?'

Poppy rolled her eyes. 'You're the boss.'

'OK, I'll do it. Be at the farm at nine o'clock sharp tomorrow. I'll soon knock her into shape.'

6

H annah was less than impressed when Poppy told her the news.

'My instructor says I have a natural talent,' she said. 'Scarlett's not going to teach me anything I don't already know.'

'I know. You are doing amazingly well, considering you only started riding last summer. You're much better than I was,' lied Poppy. 'But it's always good to have extra time in the saddle. And if Scarlett lets you ride Flynn it means we can all go out together. Will you give it a go?'

'Oh alright. But if she starts bossing me about I'm outta there.'

Hannah was even less impressed when she saw Scarlett leading a roly poly Flynn in from the field the next morning. He was still holding on stubbornly to the last clumps of his winter coat. His mane was tangled and there were several burrs in his tail. Even Poppy, who would always have a soft spot for the dark bay gelding, had to admit he did look a bit scruffy.

'He's tiny!' cried Hannah. 'I'm far too big for him.' She

pointed to the field, where Scarlett's leggy chestnut gelding Red stood dozing by the gate. 'He's more my size. Can't I ride him?'

'He's only just turned five. He's too much for you,' said Scarlett.

'But -'

'Everyone knows you should never pair two novices together,' Scarlett replied bossily. 'Flynn may be small but he's a native pony and he's well able to carry your weight, and he's the perfect schoolmaster. It's him or nothing.'

Poppy nudged Hannah. 'I learnt to ride on Flynn, too.'

Hannah cast one last longing look at Red. 'Alright,' she said eventually. She rubbed Flynn's forehead and he nibbled her pocket, looking for a treat. 'He has got a very kind face,' she conceded. 'Just don't post any photos of me riding him on Instagram otherwise Cassie'll take the mickey. She rides a gorgeous Danish Warmblood.'

Scarlett muttered something under her breath and handed Hannah a dandy brush. 'I don't suppose you've ever groomed a pony at that posh riding school of yours, have you?'

'I have, actually,' Hannah replied archly. 'At Pony Club you learn all about horse and pony care and stable management. I've just completed my Silver Award.'

'Bully for you.' Scarlett checked her watch. 'You've got twenty minutes while I lunge Red to get him looking respectable. So I should get on with it if I were you.'

Hannah set to work on Flynn and Poppy went in search of a scrubbing brush so she could clean the water trough. By the time she'd finished Flynn was a different pony. His once-tufty coat looked sleek and his bushy mane had been tamed. Hannah had even oiled his hooves.

'Good job,' said Poppy, impressed.

'Thanks. I wanted to show Miss Bossy that I'm not as useless as she thinks. Surely even she can't find fault?'

Scarlett appeared with a cavesson bridle and lunge rein in one hand and a lunge whip in the other. 'Haven't you tacked him up yet?' she said impatiently.

Hannah was indignant. 'You just told me to groom him. You didn't say anything about tacking up.'

'I'd have thought it was blindingly obvious,' tutted Scarlett.

Poppy, who was growing tired of her friends' constant bickering, made a beeline for the wheelbarrow. 'I'm going to make a start on the poo picking. I'll leave you two to it.'

SCARLETT WAS as good as her word and had Hannah on the lunge rein, barking instructions at her like a particularly hectoring sergeant major. 'Hands upright! Thumbs on top! Close your fingers! Your toes are sticking out again! Look forwards, not down! Don't hollow your back!'

Poppy found it exhausting from her vantage point in the field. Goodness knows how Hannah was taking it. But her friend's jaw was set as she did what she was told, obviously determined to prove her ability. By the time Poppy had finished poo picking and had mucked out Red's stable, Scarlett was unclipping the lunge rein from Flynn's cavesson noseband and a crimson-cheeked Hannah was patting the gelding's damp neck.

'How did it go?' asked Poppy nervously.

'She's developed a few bad habits but nothing I can't sort out,' said Scarlett, whose voice was a little raspy from all the shouting.

'Scarlett is certainly very... how shall I put it... *assertive*,' said Hannah, jumping off. 'And Flynn is like a little gorgeous teddy bear. I love him.'

'But you're happy to carry on with the lessons?' pressed Poppy.

'I suppose,' said Hannah.

'If we must,' said Scarlett.

Poppy raised one eyebrow. 'That's good. I think.'

7

The next few days fell into some kind of a routine. Every morning Poppy and Hannah crossed the field to Ashworthy where Scarlett gave Hannah a half-hour lesson on Flynn while Poppy mucked out and poo picked. In the afternoons they went for long rides on the moor, showing Hannah all their favourite places.

Hannah and Scarlett continued to bicker at every opportunity and Poppy would find herself refereeing their squabbles several times a day.

'I've decided to become a United Nations peacekeeper when I leave school. It'll be a bit less fraught than trying to stop Hannah and Scarlett's non-stop arguing,' Poppy told Caroline one afternoon.

'Now you know how I feel when you and Charlie quarrel,' her stepmum laughed. 'Annoying, isn't it?'

Even after a few days Hannah was much more relaxed in the saddle. She had fallen in love with the irrepressible Flynn, shrieking with laughter when he threw in a buck at the start of a canter or when he plunged his head down to tear at the soft spring grass halfway along a bridleway.

'She's impossible,' grumbled Scarlett, looking back at Hannah, who was letting Flynn nibble the frothy white cow parsley heads as she trailed behind them.

'But she loves Flynn,' Poppy pointed out.

Scarlett nodded reluctantly. 'Her one and only redeeming feature, in my humble opinion.'

HALFWAY through the week they were sitting on a wide, flat boulder at the top of the Riverdale tor, enjoying the view while their ponies nibbled the wiry moorland grass, when Poppy's phone pinged. Hannah grabbed it and squinted at the screen.

'Someone called Sam has sent you a really long text. Who's she? You've not mentioned her.'

'Sam is a *he*, actually,' hooted Scarlett, waggling her eyebrows at Hannah.

'You definitely didn't mention *him*,' said Hannah. 'So come on, 'fess up. Who is he?'

'Just a friend. Of mine *and* Scarlett's actually,' said Poppy, shooting Scarlett a venomous look.

'You know Poppy and I have lessons with Bella Thompson at Redhall?' said Scarlett, impervious to the dagger looks she was getting. 'Sam is Bella's grandson.'

'Is he tall, dark and handsome?' said Hannah.

'No, he's quite tall, blond and -' Poppy paused and shrugged. 'I don't know. He's just Sam.'

She lunged for her phone but Hannah threw it to Scarlett, who caught it neatly and, when Poppy tried to grab it from her, lobbed it back to Hannah. She tapped in Poppy's passcode, tucked a strand of hair behind her ear and read the text aloud.

'"Hi Poppy, how's things? Missed you and Scarlett on Wednesday. Gran gave me a lesson instead. We're still waiting to hear if we've made the team. I hope so. Star is jumping out of her skin at the moment. Did you know there's an open day at Eaglestone Arabians tomorrow? Scott and I are going. Maybe see you there? Sam." Smiley face. No kiss. What's Eaglestone Arabians?'

'It's a stud up towards Okehampton,' said Scarlett. 'It's a bit like Willy Wonka's Chocolate Factory, only there's no chocolate, just beautiful Arabian horses. The owner made a mint from a load of casinos on the south coast. He's supposed to be well dodgy.'

'Why's it like Willy Wonka's Chocolate Factory?' Hannah asked.

Scarlett widened her eyes and beckoned them closer. 'It's all very secretive. Nobody ever goes in, and nobody ever comes out.'

'So why's he suddenly decided to invite everyone along to an open day?' said Poppy.

'Who cares?' said Scarlett. 'I'd love to go and have a look around. Shall we go?'

Poppy tried to grab her phone again, but Hannah held it high in the air.

'Oo, yeah, it sounds like fun,' she said. 'And I'll get to meet the quite tall and blond Sam.'

'*And* Bella's godson, Scott, who definitely *is* tall, dark and handsome,' said Scarlett, winking.

'Can we go, Poppy, pretty please?' pleaded Hannah.

Poppy made a final lunge for her phone, plucked it out of Hannah's hand and stuffed it in her pocket.

'Well?' demanded Scarlett, her hands on her hips. 'Are we going or what?'

Poppy had the distinct feeling that, after being at loggerheads with each other for days, Hannah and Scarlett were now ganging up on her. Typical.

'I guess,' she said weakly. 'If Caroline is happy to take us.'

8

'Are we nearly there?' whined Charlie.

Caroline glanced at the sat nav. 'I think so. It's left up here somewhere.'

'I'll ask that bloke,' said Hannah, pointing to a lone figure trudging along the grass verge. Caroline pulled over and Hannah wound down her window.

'Excuse me, do you know where the Arab stud is?' she called.

A teenage boy with a mess of black hair, a pale face and eyes the colour of damp moss, bent towards the open window.

'I'm looking for it myself,' he said in a lilting Irish accent. 'The fella from the petrol station said it was a couple of miles down here. Said I couldn't miss it.'

He shifted the enormous rucksack on his back.

'That looks heavy,' said Caroline. 'Hop in. We'll give you a lift.'

'Ah sure, it's no bother. I can walk,' said the boy.

'Nonsense.' Caroline glanced at Poppy, Scarlett and Charlie in the back. 'Squash up, you three,' she ordered.

Poppy, who was closest, rolled her eyes and opened the door. The boy gave her an apologetic smile and sat down, hugging his rucksack close to his chest.

'I'm Caroline,' said Caroline. 'And this is Hannah, Poppy, Charlie and Scarlett.'

'Cameron,' said the boy. 'Nice to meet you.'

'So what brings you to this neck of the woods, Cameron?' said Scarlett.

He shrugged. 'I was passing through.'

'Passing through to *where?*' said Hannah, swivelling around to face him. 'We're in the back of beyond!'

'Ah, you know.' His eyebrows knotted. 'Cornwall.'

'Are you a hitchhiker?' said Charlie, staring at him with undisguised fascination. He shot a look at Caroline. 'Dad said you should never give lifts to hitchhikers in case they end up murdering you and stealing all your money.'

'Charlie!' said Poppy, turning crimson. Honestly, he was so embarrassing.

A shadow crossed Cameron's face and he narrowed his eyes and stared out of the window. Poppy knew she was being fanciful but it was as if the temperature in the car had plummeted ten degrees.

'Don't worry, I would never steal from anyone,' he said in a heavy voice.

'Of course you wouldn't,' said Caroline cheerfully.

Poppy elbowed her brother in the ribs. 'Idiot!' she hissed.

As the car trundled along the lane she cast sidelong glances at Cameron. She guessed he was in Year 12, so sixteen, maybe seventeen. He had a thin face but a square jawline. The type that authors would describe as *chiselled*. Lean and lanky, like teenage boys often are. As though he'd been pulled out of shape like one of those stretchy yellow men you found in party bags when you were little. There was a stillness about him that Poppy found unnerving, until she noticed his long tapering fingers, which were constantly playing with the straps of his rucksack.

He looked up and caught Poppy's eye. She blushed again. It was as if he'd known she was watching him. She took out her phone and pretended to check for messages.

'This must be it,' said Caroline, flicking on the indicator. Ahead was a pair of double gates and an ornate sign on which *Eaglestone Arabians* was etched in swirly writing over the silhouette of a prancing Arab horse. Brightly-coloured bunting, fixed to sturdy post and rail fencing, fluttered in the wind. A steward wearing a fluorescent jacket waved them into a field of parked cars.

'Thanks for the lift,' said Cameron, holding out his hand to Caroline.

'No problem. It was good to meet you.'

'Thanks for not murdering us,' grinned Charlie.

Cameron gave an ironic smile. 'Anytime.' He held up a hand in a mock salute and strode off, joining a trickle of people heading towards a cluster of farm buildings up ahead. The McKeevers, Scarlett and Hannah followed.

'Now he's interesting,' said Hannah.

Scarlett agreed. 'Very brooding. Wonder what he's doing here.'

'Same as us, I should think,' said Poppy.

As they passed a menage another steward handed her a programme.

'Eddie Eaglestone is giving a talk in the main yard at ten,' she read. She checked her watch. 'That's ten minutes.'

'I wonder where the dry ski slope is,' said Charlie, squinting into the sun.

'Ski slope?'

'For practicing his ski jumps on. Durr.'

'Why would he -' Realisation dawned. 'He's Eddie Eaglestone, not Eddie the Eagle, you twit!'

'Oh,' said Charlie, deflated. 'I wouldn't have come if I'd known that. I thought he might hold tryouts for the next Olympic ski jumping team. I was going to give it a go.'

'But you've never even skied!' said Poppy.

Charlie shrugged. 'How hard can it be?'

'Who *is* Eddie the Eagle, anyway?' asked Scarlett.

'You must have heard of him,' said Hannah. 'He was Britain's most famous Olympic ski jumper. Actually, Britain's *only* Olympic ski jumper. They made a film about him. I went to see it with my mates. But perhaps it didn't reach deepest, darkest Devon.'

'It sounds rubbish. I wouldn't have gone if it did,' said Scarlett, glaring at Hannah.

'Be nice, you two,' said Poppy. She looked around for something to distract them. 'Oh look!' she cried. 'Foals!'

Sure enough, in the paddock between the menage and the stable yard, three sleek Arab mares grazed while foals skittered by their sides, spooked by the sight of so many visitors to their usually tranquil home.

'Aren't they just *gorgeous*?' Poppy enthused. An iron grey foal with a dished face and gangly legs trotted towards the fence, his head high and his nostrils flared. Poppy held out a hand and clicked her tongue but the foal tossed his exquisite head and cantered off to the safety of his dam.

'Very sweet,' said Scarlett.

'Super cute,' said Hannah.

'Thank goodness. Something we all agree on.' Poppy linked arms with them both. 'Come on, you two. Let's go and meet their owner.'

9

The yard at Eaglestone Arabians was vast. Stables lined all four sides and in the middle was a huge square of lawned grass so green and uniform that Poppy had to pull up a handful to check it wasn't artificial. It wasn't. Beautiful Arab horses watched them from their immaculate weatherboarded stables and the concrete was spotless, with not a wisp of hay or a flake of shavings out of place. It reminded Poppy of the top-class racing stables she'd seen photos of in Horse and Hound.

A semi-circle of foldable chairs had been set up in the middle of the lawn.

'I don't believe it,' said Scarlett. 'There's Georgia La-di-da Canning.'

Poppy followed her gaze. Sure enough, Georgia was sitting in the front row, flanked by two familiar-looking girls with shiny hair and braying voices.

'Who's Georgia La-di-da Canning?' said Hannah, intrigued.

'She's the one whose parents won the lottery and bought

a huge great mansion over Tavistock way. Though they've spent most of their money now,' said Scarlett.

'Remember I told you about her? She's the one who was kidnapped,' Poppy whispered.

Hannah's face cleared. 'Yeah, I remember. You said she and Scarlett don't get on. She sounds like fun. In fact I might go and introduce myself. I have a feeling we might have a lot in common.'

'You're welcome to each other,' said Scarlett darkly.

Poppy fought the urge to bang their heads together. Instead she scanned the rest of the rows. Cameron had chosen a chair in the furthest corner of the back row. Spying two familiar faces sitting beside him, she took a deep breath and said in a careless voice, 'Look, there's Sam and Scott.'

Georgia temporarily forgotten, Hannah made a beeline for them, beckoning Poppy and Scarlett to follow her.

'Hi again Cameron,' she said. 'And you must be Sam. I'm Hannah.'

'Nice to meet you. Hey Poppy, glad you could make it,' said Sam, pushing his blond fringe out of his eyes.

Poppy felt Hannah watching her and shrugged. 'It sounded interesting.'

Scott flashed them a grin.

'This is Scott. He's a working pupil at a showjumping yard in Exeter. Remember we told you about him?' Scarlett said breathlessly.

'The tall, dark and handsome one!' said Hannah.

'That's me,' Scot twinkled. The two girls twinkled back. Charlie muttered something about needing a bucket.

'Good, there's something else you've got in common,' Poppy said briskly. She peered at Scott. 'You've had your tooth fixed.'

Scott smiled ruefully at Hannah. 'Poppy always was immune to my considerable charms.'

Scarlett bagged the chair next to Scott and Poppy found herself sandwiched between Hannah and Charlie as a man with a microphone in one hand and an adoring spaniel at his heels strode onto the grass.

'Is that Eddie-not-the-Eagle?' said Charlie.

Poppy nodded. 'It must be. Now shush and listen.'

Eddie Eaglestone reminded Poppy of a wily fox, with bright, penetrating eyes, a weathered face that had obviously never felt a drop of suntan lotion and a thatch of hair dyed an unlikely russet brown. He was wearing a pair of breeches the colour of custard, black buckled shoes, a claret-coloured cravat, a tartan waistcoat and a tweed hacking jacket, topped off with a matching deerstalker hat. He may have been aspiring to play the part of a country gent but he actually looked as if he'd been let loose in the costume wardrobe of a local am dram group.

Once everyone was seated he tapped his microphone a couple of times and beamed at them all.

'Welcome, welcome! I am so glad you could come to the first ever open day at Eaglestone Arabians. In a moment you will meet some of our beautiful horses, including our mighty stallion Eaglestone Fearless Flight, but first I wanted to talk to you about the stud and its work.' He tapped his nose. 'And then I have a *very* important announcement to make.'

Poppy zoned out as Eddie Eaglestone described how he'd found the farm a decade before and had spent thousands renovating the buildings, replacing old grain stores with new stabling, installing horse walkers and foaling boxes and filling his paddocks with the best brood mares money could buy.

She imagined what it would be like to ride an Arabian stallion like Flight through the foothills of the Persian mountains to the shores of the Caspian Sea. He would have wide-set, dark, expressive eyes, a dished face and the floatiest trot.

A long, arching neck and small, curved ears. He would be faster than the desert wind and braver than a mountain lion. It sounded impossibly romantic.

She was brought back to the present by a sharp dig in the ribs. 'Poppy, stop daydreaming,' whispered Hannah through the corner of her mouth. 'Look, that must be Fearless Flight.'

The mighty stallion, his gleaming chestnut coat like burnished gold, pranced onto the grass, led by a stud groom with legs as bowed as a jockey's and nicotine-stained fingers.

'I'm known as a gambling man, but the biggest gamble I ever took was on a two-year-old colt eight years ago,' said Eddie Eaglestone. 'His bloodlines could be traced back to the Bedouin Arabians, who were bred for their intelligence, courage and endurance. And here he is, with my head groom and right hand man, Micky Murphy.'

The stallion tossed his noble head and watched them intently, an aristocrat among horses.

'Fearless Flight has lived up to his name. He has sired a generation of fearless, noble horses who have made their name both in the show ring and as endurance horses. Thank you, Micky.' There was a quiet ripple of applause as the stud groom led the stallion away.

'And here, I am delighted to say, is the newest addition to Flight's tribe,' said Eddie Eaglestone.

Everyone sighed with pleasure as another groom led a plump chestnut mare with a chestnut foal at foot onto the grass. The colt was a mini version of his blue-blooded sire, even down to his flaxen mane and tail and his patrician bearing as he stood at his dam's side.

'I have loved Arab horses ever since I watched the epic film Lawrence of Arabia as a young man. Then, ten years ago, I set out to have the best Arabian stud the West Country had ever seen. I am sure you will agree I have achieved that aim and that our horses here at Eaglestone Arabians are the most beautiful in the world.'

There were general murmurs of assent. Eddie Eaglestone cleared his throat. 'And now I come to the most important announcement of all. A competition the like of which you have never seen before. A competition with a once-in-a-lifetime prize. A competition that will blow your mind!'

'Maybe it's to win an Arab!' Poppy whispered excitedly. Scarlett and Hannah were both leaning forward, their elbows on their knees and their chins resting in their hands, their eyes glued to the flamboyant stud owner.

'I have devised a treasure hunt to celebrate the tenth anniversary of Eaglestone Arabians. It will require competitors to demonstrate the intelligence, energy and tenacity of an Arabian horse. And it is a treasure hunt with a difference. A treasure hunt on horseback, and the prize is a golden horse!'

'A real horse?' cried a girl with pigtails sitting in front of Poppy.

Eddie Eaglestone laughed. 'No, not a real horse. But just as exciting.' He bent down to retrieve a clay casket at his feet and reached inside. 'This is the treasure competitors will be searching for,' he said, holding a small prancing golden horse in the palm of his hand.

'It's an amulet, a dancing Arabian stallion, cast by a local craftsman just for this competition.' He held the amulet aloft. Everyone watched, rapt, as it sparkled in the sunlight.

'It will be buried in its clay casket to ward off -'

'Evil spirits?' called Scott.

Eddie Eaglestone looked down his long nose at Scott. 'Metal detector enthusiasts.'

There was a ripple of laughter.

'The treasure hunt is open to teams of three riders. The first clue will be sent by text to the team leader at precisely ten o'clock on Friday morning. Teams will have two days to complete the challenge, camping here on Friday night. The hunt for the golden horse will take you across the moor, from one clue to another. But time will be of the essence. The team that cracks all the clues first will find their just reward. There will be a prizegiving ceremony here at four o'clock on Saturday afternoon.'

Charlie was on the edge of his seat. 'How much is the golden horse worth?'

Poppy blushed in embarrassment but Eddie Eaglestone just laughed. 'I like your directness, young man. Any other questions?'

Sam raised a hand. 'Who can enter?'

'As a thank you to you all for showing such an interest in my beloved horses I have decided to restrict entries to people here today. For health and safety reasons the minimum age of team members is thirteen.'

Charlie groaned.

'And now for the small print,' said Eddie Eaglestone, placing the golden amulet carefully back in its clay casket. 'Under eighteens must have parental consent. Camping equipment can be dropped off at the stud on Friday morning and water will be provided for horses and riders. Entrants must agree to media interviews and sign a waiver confirming that they understand they are taking part at their own risk.'

The stud owner smiled benevolently at them all and clapped his hands. 'And you need to be quick. Registration closes in precisely fifteen minutes!'

Scarlett jumped to her feet. 'Let's enter a team! It'll be so cool!'

'What, the three of us?' said Poppy doubtfully.

'The Three Amigos!' cried Hannah. 'Awesome idea!'

'The Three Amigos?' Poppy spluttered. 'You two never stop bickering!'

'Ah, but we wouldn't on the treasure hunt, would we, Hannah?' said Scarlett.

'Absolutely not. It would give us a common purpose. We would have to work together.'

'But we don't have a tent.'

'We do. Mum and Dad bought Alex one for his Duke of Edinburgh Gold Award. We can use that,' said Scarlett.

'I'd *love* to go,' said Charlie.

'Well, no-one's asking you. I don't know. A priceless golden horse and a treasure hunt that only people here today can enter? It all sounds a bit…far-fetched,' Poppy said lamely.

Scarlett rolled her eyes. 'Don't be wet, Poppy.'

Hannah stood beside Scarlett looking down at her. 'Yeah, where's your sense of adventure?'

If Poppy found Hannah and Scarlett's constant quarrelling irritating, she realised that she liked them ganging up on her even less.

'Eddie Eaglestone said we need parental consent,' she said weakly.

Caroline, who had been listening to their conversation, leant forward and patted Poppy's knee. 'It sounds like great fun. I think you should do it. And I'm sure Sarah will agree. I'll text her now.'

Poppy chewed a nail. It wasn't that she didn't like the sound of a treasure hunt on horseback, it was just that she hated things being sprung on her without notice. She liked to be able to plan ahead, prepare for things. She liked advance warning.

'We'd enter a team but we're one short,' said Sam.

Charlie bowed and said gravely, 'Charles Henry McKeever, at your service.'

Sam patted him on the back. 'Charlie, that would be great, only -'

'- you're too young!' Poppy finished in exasperation.

'I'll join your team,' a voice said casually.

They turned to see Cameron, leaning back in his chair as if he hadn't a care in the world. Only Poppy noticed those long, elegant fingers of his were still worrying at the strap of his rucksack.

Scott looked the Irish boy up and down.

'Can you ride?'

'Sure, I've been riding since I was tiny. I've hunted back home for years.'

Scott looked impressed. 'Well, if you've hunted in Ireland I'd say you must be pretty competent.'

'We can vouch for Cameron,' said Charlie. 'He's definitely not a murderer, anyway.'

Scott grinned and glanced at Sam. 'What d'you reckon, Samantha? He can ride and he's not going to murder us. Have we found ourselves a team-mate?'

Sam offered Cameron his hand. 'Welcome to the A-Team. Where d'you keep your horse?'

Cameron ran a hand through his unruly hair. 'Ah, I probably should have mentioned that. The thing is, I don't actually have one.'

Sam smiled his easy smile. 'It's a good job my Gran has a riding school then, isn't it? Horses are the one thing we're not short of.'

Scarlett clapped her hands in satisfaction. 'That's you sorted. We just need Poppy to agree now.'

They all looked at her expectantly. If she said no she would be the party pooper, the stuffed shirt, the miserable killjoy spoiling everyone's fun. 'Alright,' she said finally. 'I'll do it.'

'Woo hoo!' shouted Scarlett, punching the air.

'Hurray!' cried Hannah, throwing her arms around Poppy.

'Cool,' said Sam, his blue eyes crinkling at the corners.

Poppy pulled herself to her feet. 'I guess we'd better go and register.'

Once they'd signed a waiver form with small print so tiny you needed a magnifying glass to read it, the three girls found a quiet corner overlooking a paddock where half a dozen leggy Arab yearlings were grazing in the spring sunshine. Poppy, who had been given the job of team leader in the hope that it would fire up some enthusiasm for the task ahead, read the set of instructions they'd been given.

'Welcome to a treasure hunt with a difference! You will need to show the intelligence, energy and tenacity of an Arabian horse -'

'Yes, yes, he said all that already. Cut to the chase,' said Hannah impatiently.

'OK, so each team leader will receive the first clue by text at precisely ten o'clock on Friday morning,' read Poppy. 'Each clue will lead us to the next. Clues will be based around famous Dartmoor landmarks and legends. We'll be given a piece of card which needs to be stamped at each clue stop to prove that we've been there. There'll be a special stamp at each stop to do that.' Poppy scanned the

A4 sheet of closely-typed paper. 'We'll all camp overnight here at the stud. We need to provide tents and our food. They'll lay on grazing for the horses, plus food, hay and water.'

'Nice,' said Scarlett.

'The last clue will lead us to the golden horse. The first team there will be declared the winners and will get to keep it.'

'How many teams do you think there are?' said Hannah.

The other two shrugged. It was hard to tell. There had been a long line of people queuing up to register but some, like Caroline and Charlie, may have been tagging along for moral support.

'At least six, maybe as many as twelve,' said Scarlett.

'That's helpful,' scoffed Hannah.

'Well, do you know how many there are, smartypants?'

Poppy held up her hand to silence them. 'Hey, you promised you wouldn't argue. All for one and one for all, and all that.'

'What?' said Scarlett.

'Eh?' said Hannah.

Poppy pictured her patience as a length of tightly-woven steel, stretched to breaking point. She exhaled slowly. 'The Three Amigos, remember? It was your idea, Hannah.'

Scarlett snorted with laughter. 'You are a twit sometimes, Poppy. You're thinking about the Three Musketeers.'

THE THREE AMIGOS sat cross-legged in Cloud's paddock the next day staring at the tangle of blue nylon, metal poles, guy ropes and tent pegs that had slithered out of the matching blue drawstring bag Scarlett had hefted across the fields from Ashworthy.

Hannah leant forward, sniffed the tent and pulled a face. 'It smells really musty.'

'It's spent the last two years in the barn. Of course it smells musty. We'll set it up now and give it a good airing. It'll be fine,' said Scarlett.

Poppy reached for a tent peg. It was as twisted as a shepherd's crook, as if Alex had tried hammering it into one of the impenetrable granite boulders that littered the moor. She gripped each end and tried to bend the peg straight, but it swivelled like a corkscrew in her hands. She gave up and tossed it back onto the pile.

'Have either of you ever actually put up a tent?' she asked doubtfully.

Hannah shook her head. 'Where we go camping in France the tents are already set up.'

'I haven't either, but honestly, how hard can it be?' Scarlett sprang to her feet and started unravelling the guy ropes. 'Well, don't just sit there,' she scolded, thrusting a tent pole into Hannah's hand and pulling Poppy to her feet.

They spent the next forty minutes wrestling with the tent poles, trying to pull them through the fabric gaps in the nylon to form the frame of the tent.

'This is useless. The poles keep coming apart,' said Poppy.

'It's a rubbish tent, that's the problem,' grumbled Hannah. 'Where did you buy it, the pound shop?'

Scarlett's eyes flashed dangerously. 'A good workman never blames his tools.'

'That's because he's never tried putting up this stupid tent,' Hannah retorted.

Ignoring her friends, Poppy pulled the poles back out of the nylon and twisted them so tightly her knuckles protested. 'One last go,' she muttered. She fed the end of the pole through its corresponding flap and started pulling it through. Just when she thought she'd nailed it the end of the pole came away in her hand and the tent crumpled to the ground like a bouncy castle being deflated at the end of a school fete.

Poppy growled and aimed a kick at the pile of poles and folds of blue nylon. 'I give up,' she declared, collapsing on the ground.

A dog barked, followed by the sound of thundering feet.

'Just when I thought things couldn't get any worse,' she groaned.

'What's up?' said Hannah, through a mouthful of tent pegs.

Poppy waved an arm in the direction of the house. 'Charlie.'

12

Freddie bounded up, his plumy tail quivering with excitement as he nosed around the tent, which smelt enticingly of mice. Charlie stood with his feet planted wide apart and his hands on his hips, his gaze flickering between the unmade tent and the flushed faces of his sister and her two friends.

'Need some help?' he said kindly.

'No,' said Poppy.

'Yes!' chorused Scarlett and Hannah.

'You know nothing about tents!' cried Poppy.

'Er, yes I do. I'm in the Cubs, remember. We put up tents all the time. I was the first in my Six to get my Outdoors Challenge Award.' He gave them all a patronising smile. 'What seems to be the problem?'

'Every time we try to pull the poles through the tent they just come apart inside and we have to pull them out and start again,' said Scarlett.

'That's because you need to push them through. I'll show you.' Charlie snapped the tent poles together and slid one end into its slot. The nylon wrinkled around the metal pole like a stocking puckering around an old lady's ankle. Charlie hummed tunelessly to himself as he fed it through, reaching the eyelet at the far side without incident.

He fed the second length of pole in, forming a cross. With a flick of his wrist the two poles bent into position. 'Now we need to peg the tent down and fix the fly sheet.'

They watched him hammer the pegs in at forty five degrees. He positioned the fly sheet in place and fastened it to the ground.

'Make sure the fly sheet and the inner tent aren't touching, otherwise the rain and condensation will leak through and you'll be wet by the morning.' Charlie staked the fly sheet to the ground and stood back to admire his handiwork. 'There you go. It's easy, see?'

He unzipped the door and scrambled inside. The three girls followed him in.

'It's tiny,' said Poppy, looking around in dismay.

'It's *cosy*,' corrected Charlie.

Hannah pinched her nose between finger and thumb. 'It's smelly.'

Scarlett shrugged. 'Take it or leave it, guys. It's all we have.'

CAROLINE OFFERED to drive the tent, their sleeping bags, pillows, food and cooking equipment over to the Eaglestone stud first thing on Friday morning.

'At least you don't have to carry everything on the ponies,' she said brightly.

Poppy, who was struggling to work up any enthusiasm for the treasure hunt, grunted, 'I s'pose.'

She sneezed loudly.

'You're not going down with something, are you?' said Caroline.

Poppy shook her head. 'Just a bit of hay fever.'

Caroline pressed a handkerchief into her hand and passed her a packet of anti-histamines and a glass of water. 'Make sure you take one before you go.'

By eight o'clock everything was packed. Charlie handed Poppy his bird-watching binoculars and his treasured Swiss Army knife.

'You never know when they might come in useful,' he said solemnly.

Poppy smiled. Charlie could be annoying, but he always meant well. 'Thanks, little bro. And thanks for your help with the tent. It's a shame you can't come, too. We'd be unbeatable with you in the team.'

Charlie's whole face lit up and Caroline flashed Poppy a grateful smile.

Poppy ruffled her brother's hair and slipped the knife and binoculars into her rucksack. For the first time since Eddie Eaglestone had announced the treasure hunt she felt a lick of excitement, like tentative flames darting and fizzing in a pile of tinder-dry kindling.

She grinned at Hannah. 'I reckon we're as ready as we'll ever be, don't you?'

Hannah high fived her and grinned back. 'You bet. Bring it on!'

13

They decided to wait for the first clue outside Waterby Post Office and Stores. Poppy's phone managed a respectable three bars if she sat on Cloud to the far side of the shop with her arm stretched skywards like a swotty kid in a classroom. The shop was on the edge of the moor, and it was perfect for stocking up on last minute snacks and treats, which was exactly what Scarlett was doing while Hannah held Red's reins.

Scarlett finally appeared, her pockets bulging.

'Honestly, I spend most of my wages in that place,' she said, ripping open a Mars bar with her teeth and taking a large bite. 'Barney might as well pay me in chocolates and sweets.'

She took Red's reins and offered Hannah a Twix.

'You're alright, thanks, I've only just cleaned my teeth,' said Hannah.

'Your loss,' said Scarlett through a mouthful of chocolate. 'Poppy?'

'Can't. My stomach's in knots.'

'What's there to be nervous about? This is supposed to be fun,' said Hannah.

'She's always like this.' Scarlett seemed pleased to have an insight into Poppy's character that Hannah didn't. 'You should have seen her before her first show. She was as white as a sheet. Anyone would have thought she'd seen a ghost.'

Poppy, who had lost all feeling in her right arm, checked her watch.

'It's five past. I bet they took my number down wrong,' she fretted.

At that moment her phone beeped. Hannah yelped in excitement, making Red skitter sideways, his eyes rolling. Scarlett, who had one foot in the stirrup and one on the ground, cursed under her breath, hopped a couple of times and heaved herself into the saddle.

Poppy stared at her phone.

'Read it, then!' cried Hannah.

'Give me a chance.' Poppy glanced at her two friends, who were watching her with eyes like hawks. 'Are you sitting comfortably?' she asked.

They both nodded impatiently.

'Then I'll begin.'

Poppy cleared her throat.

> 'The first clue you'll find
> In a tree ancient and true
> In the shadow of St Mary
> I can see it - can yew?'

Hannah rode Flynn alongside Cloud and grabbed Poppy's phone. Her lips worked as she read the riddle to herself. Scarlett's face was scrunched up in concentration.

It seemed obvious to Poppy. If the clues were all this easy they'd have found the amulet before dusk. 'I'd say we're looking for an old yew tree in St Mary's Churchyard, wouldn't you?'

'Oh yes,' said Scarlett, her face clearing. 'Silly me.'

'How far is it?' said Hannah, tightening her reins.

Poppy laughed. 'About four hundred metres in that direction,' she said, pointing to the spire which peeked out from behind a line of oak trees. 'There's a massive yew tree with a plaque on it in the churchyard. It must be that one.'

Hannah turned Flynn towards the church and kicked him into a trot. She turned back to them, her eyes shining. 'So what are we waiting for?'

THE CHURCHYARD WAS empty bar a couple of sparrows who were pecking hopefully in the dust in front of the old oak doors. Poppy jumped off Cloud and reached in her rucksack for the piece of card she'd been given when they signed up for the treasure hunt. It was marked into a grid of six squares, one for each of the six clues.

'The tree's right at the back.' Poppy beckoned the others to follow her along a gravel path that ducked and weaved through lichen-covered headstones to the far corner of the churchyard. They stood in the shadow of the ancient yew and gazed up at the branches laden with forest-green needles.

'It's over a thousand years old. Charlie told me,' said Poppy.

Scarlett slithered off Red and grabbed a small wooden box that was dangling from a chain wrapped around the trunk of the yew. Inside were a stamp and an ink pad. Poppy passed her card and Scarlett stamped the first square. She peered at the red inky blob.

'Cool. It's a tiny picture of an Arab horse.'

'One down, five to go. And we're in the lead already,' Hannah crowed.

'More by luck than judgement,' said Poppy. 'I wonder where the next clue is?'

Scarlett peered into the box again. 'It's written inside:

'Two arms, but fingers I have none.
Two feet, yet I cannot run.
Strong as an ox, I'll carry your load.
Come and find my humble abode.'

Scarlett replaced the lid of the box and jumped back in the saddle. 'What d'you reckon, is it old Arthur's prizewinning bull?'

Poppy giggled. 'I hope not. You can go into his field and get the stamp if it is. No, that's too obvious. We've got to think outside the box, literally and metaphorically.'

'A clock has two hands and a face,' said Hannah.

'A chair has arms and legs but no head,' said Poppy.

'None of which are getting us any closer to solving the riddle.' Scarlett sighed. 'This one's *way* harder.'

'What carries a load?' said Hannah.

Scarlett chewed the end of her finger. 'A lorry? A train?'

'A donkey?' said Poppy, picturing Chester and Jenny as they'd watched her push a barrowload of manure from the field to the muck heap the previous afternoon. 'But donkeys can run, so it can't be a donkey.' A grin spread slowly across her face. 'I think I know what it is.'

14

Scarlett and Hannah stared at Poppy.

'Well?' Scarlett demanded.

'It's a wheelbarrow, isn't it? They've got arms and feet *and* they carry a load.'

'But wheelbarrows don't have houses,' said Hannah. 'Pass me the map, will you?'

As Poppy fished the map out of her rucksack she wracked her brains for inspiration but the harder she tried to think, the emptier her head became.

Hannah stabbed the map with her index finger. 'There's a Barrow Tor there, look. Could that be it?'

'Of course!' cried Scarlett, clapping her palm against her forehead. 'Why didn't I think of that. D'you remember, Poppy? That old shepherd's croft? We had a picnic there once.'

Poppy did remember. With only three walls still standing, the croft was little more than a ruin. But the old walls provided the perfect wind break and the view of the moor was amazing.

'How far is it?' said Hannah.

Poppy was already checking her girth and springing into the saddle. 'About an hour and a half, I should think.'

'So let's go!'

The three ponies clattered down the lane, Red and Cloud in front with Flynn bustling along behind them. Cloud felt fresh and zinging with energy. When they turned off the lane onto the moor he crabbed sideways, snatching at his bit.

'Let's canter,' Poppy called to the others, giving the Connemara his head and crouching low over the saddle as his long strides covered the ground. Despite the rucksack on her back she felt as weightless as a bird, like a buzzard floating on thermals. Beside her Red's flaxen mane ruffled in the breeze and he stretched his neck out, trying to inch his nose in front of Cloud. Behind, Hannah chattered to Flynn, urging him to keep up with the bigger ponies. Above, the late spring sun warmed the back of their necks, reminding them that summer was just around the corner. If anyone could bottle happiness, Poppy thought, this would be it.

After a while Hannah and Flynn started lagging behind.

'I keep forgetting Flynn's not as fit as our two,' Poppy said, sitting back in the saddle and easing Cloud into a trot. Once he was walking she let the reins slide through her fingers so he could stretch his neck. They were climbing steadily, following an old railway track that ran all the way to Jackman's Quarry. Black-faced sheep darted out of their way and Dartmoor ponies watched them as they passed.

When they reached the old quarry they turned sharp left.

'That's Barrow Tor,' said Scarlett, pointing to the huge tor in front of them. At the summit stood a mass of rock as grey as the lead in one of Poppy's pencils. 'People say it looks a bit like a wheelbarrow from certain angles, hence the name.'

Hannah narrowed her eyes and gazed at the cairn. 'It looks like a large lump of granite to me.'

'Let's walk the last bit. Give the ponies a breather,' said Poppy, holding her reins in one hand and swinging her leg over Cloud's hindquarters, landing on the grass with a thud. Scarlett and Hannah followed suit and they picked their way through the rocky ground, jumping from tussock to tussock in the waterlogged patches of ground where the peaty mire threatened to squelch over their jodhpur boots. By the time they reached the top they were all out of breath. Hannah leant against Flynn's flank and stared at the sweeping panorama below.

She whistled. 'Wow, that's some view.'

'Better than the view from Richmond Park?' said Poppy.

Hannah nodded. 'It's like the play mat I had when I was a kid. D'you remember, Poppy? We used to play horses versus dinosaurs on it.'

'Do we really have time for reminiscing? We're supposed to be on a treasure hunt,' said Scarlett.

Poppy ignored her. 'I remember! I used to love that game. As long as the horses didn't get gored by the Triceratops.'

'Happy times,' chuckled Hannah.

'They were,' Poppy agreed.

Noticing that Scarlett had gone quiet, Poppy pointed out the many landmarks she recognised. Dartmoor Prison, the reservoir at Spinney Bridge, the thick belt of conifers that guarded Witch Cottage, Riverdale's tor, George Blackstone's ramshackle farm.

'See those two cottages to the right of the farm? That's where the kidnappers kept Georgia Canning. But we found her and rescued her, didn't we, Scar?'

Scarlett grunted.

'And I think that's Redhall Equestrian Centre over there. That's where Scarlett and I have our weekly riding lessons.'

'And where Sam lives?' said Hannah.

'Technically he lives with his mum just down the road,

but he spends most of his time at Redhall, so I suppose you could say he does. Couldn't you, Scar?'

Scarlett grunted again. Poppy stole a look at her best friend. She was playing with a strand of Red's mane with a nonchalant air, although the rigid set of her shoulders gave her away. *I'm trying to include you*, Poppy told her silently.

Beside her Hannah stiffened. 'Oh no!'

'What's up?'

'There's another team, look!'

Poppy shielded her eyes from the sun. 'I can't see them.'

'There!'

Poppy looked again. This time she saw three riders cantering along the railway track, as tiny as ants. She reached inside her rucksack for Charlie's binoculars, adjusted the focus and zoomed in. 'I think it's Sam, Scott and Cameron.'

Scarlett exhaled in frustration. 'I *told* you we were wasting time. We need to go.' She jumped on Red and trotted around the cairn and out of sight.

Hannah raised her eyebrows. 'What's up with her?'

'She's got a point. We don't want them to see us, otherwise they'll just follow us to the next clue.'

Scarlett had already reached the old croft by the time they caught her up. They found the wooden box hidden in what remained of the chimney breast. Scarlett stamped their card and stared at the clue in the bottom of the box.

'Well?' said Hannah.

'I've memorised it. Let's get going.'

They were riding down the opposite side of Barrow Tor when Hannah patted her pockets and pulled Flynn up. 'I must have dropped my phone when we stopped. Won't be a sec.'

She handed her reins to Poppy and dashed out of sight. Seconds later she was back, waving her phone in her hand.

'Come *on*, Hannah,' Scarlett said. 'They're going to catch us up otherwise.'

Hannah cackled. 'Actually, Scarlett O'Hara, that's where you're wrong.'

carlett swung around in the saddle to face Hannah. 'What d'you mean, that's where I'm wrong?'

Hannah looked shifty. Poppy felt her stomach clench.

'What have you done?'

'Just given us a bit of a head start.' Hannah waved her hand airily.

'What do you mean?' Scarlett said again, her voice grim.

'There was a ledge hidden inside the chimney. I suppose it must have been where they baked bread in the olden days. I hid the box on the ledge. It'll take them ages to find it.'

'That's cheating!' cried Scarlett.

'It's not fair on the other teams,' said Poppy. 'You need to go and put it back, Hannah. Now.'

Hannah pulled a face. 'Oh, get over yourselves. Don't you think the others aren't above a bit of gamesmanship? They'll find the box.' She chuckled to herself. 'Eventually.'

'I think you're well and truly out of order.' Scarlett shook her head in disbelief and kicked Red into a trot. 'I'm going,' she shouted over her shoulder.

Poppy stared at Scarlett's retreating back, torn between her two friends. Beside her Hannah was muttering under her breath, 'I was only trying to help.'

Glancing down the valley, Poppy could see Sam, Scott and Cameron heading closer. Cloud stamped his foot impatiently and she tightened her reins.

Hannah tutted. 'Scarlett's such a sanctimonious -'

Poppy cut across her. 'For the record, I don't approve either. If we win, I want it to be fair and square. So don't pull another stunt like that, alright?'

Hannah shrugged sulkily. 'Whatever.'

They caught up with Scarlett at the base of the tor.

'Hey Scar, how do you know you're going in the right direction?' said Poppy.

'Yeah, you still haven't told us the next clue,' said Hannah.

'I know I'm going in the right direction because I've worked out the riddle.'

'So, what was the clue, smarty pants?' said Hannah.

Scarlett shot her a filthy look and addressed Poppy.

> *'Four legs beat two*
> *When you're planning a steal.*
> *Stand and deliver*
> *Or we don't have a deal.'*

'Dick Turpin!' said Hannah triumphantly.

Scarlett rolled her eyes. 'Dick Turpin never came to Dartmoor, you idiot. It'll be Highwayman's Hill, at Stoney Cross. They used to hang highwaymen from a gibbet at the crossroads as a warning to others, Dad told me. They've recreated the gibbet and there's one of those information panels about highwaymen next to it. The tourists love the gruesome stories about the public executions. I reckon that's where the next clue is.'

'How far from here?' said Poppy.

'Only about three miles.'

'So what are we waiting for?' cried Hannah.

As they rode further along the valley Poppy pulled Cloud close to Red. She leant over and touched Scarlett's arm.

'I'm sorry, Scar. I know Hannah can be a bit…impetuous sometimes. But her heart's in the right place.'

Scarlett raised her eyebrows. 'If you say so. But you know what happened to cheats in the olden days, if they were found guilty of treason?'

'No.'

'They were hung, drawn and quartered and their remains were displayed in a gibbet for the world to see.' Scarlett frowned. 'Although that would be too good for Hannah if you ask me.'

Poppy sighed. 'Honestly, you two are as bad as each other.'

THERE ARE companionable silences and awkward silences. And this silence was definitely of the awkward variety, Poppy decided, as she followed Scarlett and Red along the banks of a stream, with Hannah and Flynn trailing behind them.

I'm piggy in the middle, she thought, not for the first time since Hannah had come to stay. It was so frustrating because Hannah and Scarlett had so much in common, if only they would admit it. They shared the same sometimes ridiculous sense of humour. They were both extroverts. Both competitive. They loved horses. Occasionally, when they forgot their antipathy towards each other, they got on like a house on fire, even ganging up on Poppy once or twice. But most of the time they bickered like recalcitrant siblings and it was getting on her nerves.

Beside them the stream gurgled and spluttered over rocks green with algae. It had been a wet spring and, like the countless other streams that criss-crossed the moor, the water level was as high as Poppy had ever seen it.

She found the muted burble of water calming, and she let her mind drift, enjoying the sun on her face and the scent of warm horse mingling with the slightly fusty smell of peaty earth. Once, she saw the iridescent blue flash of a kingfisher's wing, but by the time she'd turned to tell Hannah the tiny bird had disappeared.

She was daydreaming about Arab stallions when Cloud stopped, sniffed the air and spun around on his hocks, his head high. Poppy ran her hand along his neck.

'Hey boy, what's up?'

He gave a high-pitched whinny. Poppy squinted into the sun, her face clearing as three riders appeared from a thicket of trees to their left. She realised she was smiling. 'It's Sam and the others. Let's wait for them.'

'Why?' cried Hannah. 'We'll lose our lead!'

'Why not?' said Scarlett, her hazel eyes sparkling. She'd had a crush on Scott from the moment they'd met. Poppy couldn't understand it - he was way too smooth, too sure of himself, for her liking. But in Scarlett's eyes he could do no wrong.

He cantered over to them on a powerful-looking iron grey gelding.

'Bella let you ride Troy?' said Poppy, surprised. The 16.2hh Irish Sport Horse was Bella's pride and joy. She'd imported him from Ireland the previous autumn after falling in love with his photo in the classified pages of Horse and Hound. Bella, whose reputation as a no-nonsense, old-school horsewoman reached across several counties, was utterly captivated by him and, in Poppy's view, let him get away with murder.

'Scott somehow convinced Gran that it'd be a good experience for him,' said Sam, riding up on his black Connemara mare, Star. Poppy knew Sam agreed with her that the big gelding was spoilt rotten.

'I'm not letting Bella hunt him until I know he's safe,' said Scott.

'He'll never be safe. He's all brawn and no brain,' said Sam.

Troy was clearly totally over-excited. His flanks were dark with sweat and he plunged forwards, his hooves cutting into the soft ground like a scythe through corn. Poppy edged Cloud away from his muscular haunches - he didn't wear a red ribbon on his tail for nothing.

Sam shook his head and sighed. 'Idiot horse.'

Cameron was riding Bella's Welsh cob Floyd. He hadn't lied about being able to ride, Poppy thought. He sat astride the sturdy liver chestnut gelding with all the easy assurance of someone who has spent much of their life in the saddle.

'So are you lot in the lead?' Scott asked.

'We were,' said Hannah pointedly.

'We were just lucky the first clue was in Waterby,' said Poppy. 'Have you seen any of the other teams?'

'A couple,' said Scott. 'There are three women on Arab endurance horses. I reckon they're our stiffest competition, but they've come from Bodmin and I don't think they know Dartmoor very well. They obviously didn't get the Barrow Tor clue because when we last saw them they were heading towards Princetown.'

'And then we saw Georgia Canning and her cronies following them,' said Sam.

'You're kidding!' Scarlett looked immensely cheered. 'Trust La-di-da Canning to cheat.'

'Are you heading to Highwayman's Hill?' Sam said quietly to Poppy as Cloud and Star touched noses.

Poppy nodded. 'Want to tag along?'

Sam looked pleased. 'Awesome. Let's hope the next box isn't quite so well-hidden as the last one. We were beginning to think we'd got the clue all wrong.'

Poppy blushed. Fortunately Sam didn't appear to notice. He stood up in his stirrups and pointed towards Stoney Cross.

'Highwayman's Hill here we come!'

16

Stoney Cross was a bleak intersection of two roads high on the moor. It was considered a fine viewpoint, and on a clear day you could see as far as Widecombe. But today the hazy sunshine obscured all but the neighbouring tors.

A narrow lane edged with acid-green bracken and pitted with potholes led them up Highwayman's Hill. They trotted up the lane, Troy and Scott a couple of lengths ahead of them and Flynn, as usual, bringing up the rear. Poppy could hear Hannah grumbling under her breath. She pulled Cloud up until Hannah and Flynn reached them.

'What's up?'

Hannah threw a look in Sam's direction. 'I know you've got a soft spot for Sam, but I don't see why that means they get to tag along.'

Poppy felt herself flushing for a second time but she kept her voice matter-of-fact. 'The more the merrier. This is supposed to be fun, remember. That's what you told me.'

'But they've stolen our lead.'

'It doesn't matter. We'll all be setting off at the same time tomorrow so actually any lead today is irrelevant. And they might be able to help with the next clue, mightn't they?'

'I doubt it,' said Hannah. She paused. 'Cameron's a bit of a mystery, isn't he?'

'What d'you mean?'

'Devon's a long way to come just to see an Arabian stud.'

'It's not as far as the Middle East. And anyway, you know what the Irish are like about their horses.'

Hannah bit her lip. 'I know. But still. I wonder why he's really here.'

'Does he have to have an ulterior motive? Perhaps he's after a job with Eddie Eaglestone.'

Hannah considered this. 'Maybe.'

'And I know he's quiet -'

'Brooding, more like.'

'- but he seems alright, doesn't he?'

They glanced ahead. Cameron was riding alongside Sam, who was pointing out the plain wooden gibbet that stood like a deathly sentry beside the crossroads.

'Yeah, he does,' Hannah conceded. 'Ignore me. I'm being silly.'

'I'm usually the one with the over-active imagination,' said Poppy. 'But I have a gut feeling that Cameron is OK.'

Hannah grinned. 'Poppy's belly has spoken. In which case I'll shut up.'

It was only as they reached Stoney Cross that Poppy realised her stomach really was talking to her. Rumbling, anyway. She checked her watch. It was almost one o'clock and breakfast seemed a long time ago.

'I'm starving. Can we have some lunch?' she said.

'Let's find the clue first,' said Scarlett. She jumped off Red and led him towards the gibbet. The box had been strung on a length of rope from the top of the wooden structure and was swaying gently in the breeze. Red snorted, rolled his eyes and planted all four feet firmly on the ground. He was going nowhere. Poppy rode Cloud alongside and took his reins.

'Just where the body would have dangled from,' said Sam. 'Someone has gallows humour.'

'Very funny, Samantha,' said Scott.

'I wonder who set the clues,' Poppy wondered.

'Who cares. What does it say?' said Hannah.

Scarlett reached for the box. 'Let me stamp our card first.'

'Do ours while you're at it,' said Scott.

'Cool, a green horse this time,' said Scarlett, stamping both cards. There were just three spaces left.

Shielding her eyes from the sun, she peered into the box and read,

> *'Pointy hat, ginger cat*
> *Secluded dell, bottomless well*
> *Black magic, endings tragic*
> *Tiny croft, I'm concealed in the loft.'*

'Eh?' said Scott.

'Black magic?' muttered Hannah.

'Read it again,' said Sam.

But Poppy and Scarlett were grinning at each other like idiots.

'Witch Cottage!' they cried.

They decided to head back to the stream for lunch so the horses could have a drink.

'This is perfect,' said Poppy, pointing to a sunny patch where a circle of boulders made for an excellent picnic spot.

'It's like someone put them here just for us,' said Hannah with satisfaction.

'To be fair, I think they've probably been here for a while,' said Sam. 'It's the remains of a Bronze Age hut by the look of it.'

Poppy ran up her stirrups, loosened Cloud's girth a couple of holes and undid the bottom strap of his grackle noseband so he could graze unhindered. She reached in her rucksack for the small bottle of water and cheese and pickle sandwich Caroline had made for her earlier. It was on the squashed side but Poppy didn't care. She took a huge bite and chewed thoughtfully.

'Witch Cottage is a long way away. I reckon it'll take the best part of two hours to get there,' she said.

Cameron, who was perched on the boulder next to hers,

glanced at the sun. 'And how far from there back to Eagle-stone Arabians?'

'At least an hour,' said Scarlett.

'Will we have time for another clue after that?' he asked.

'Probably not,' said Scott.

'Scott's got a hot date tonight,' Sam explained.

'You're not camping? said Scarlett, barely bothering to disguise her disappointment.

''Fraid not, Scarlett. Which is just as well, because Cameron doesn't have a tent either. He's going to share with Sam.'

Cameron's long black fringe hid his face as he rifled through his rucksack. As he did a folded piece of paper fluttered out, dancing on the breeze like a mayfly and landing at Poppy's feet.

She picked it up and, without thinking, smoothed it open. 'Oh!' she exclaimed. 'How beautiful.' It was a photocopy of a picture of an Arab colt. His head was high and his eyes like deep pools as he gazed straight at the camera. Poppy couldn't tell what colour he was as the photocopy was black and white, but her eyes were drawn to the perfect diamond-shaped star in the middle of his forehead. He had four identical white socks, as if he'd been dipped in a vat of white paint.

'He's stunning,' she said, handing the piece of paper back to Cameron. 'Is he yours?'

The Irish boy shook his head abruptly. Was it Poppy's imagination, or had his face grown even paler than normal?

'Did I say something wrong?'

'No. Don't make a fuss. It's just a picture.' Cameron shoved it roughly back into his rucksack.

'It's OK, boys are allowed to like horses you know. Look at those two,' Poppy waved an arm at Sam and Scott, who were trying to settle an argument over which horse was the greatest ever showjumper of all time, Ryan's Son or Milton.

'It's not that. I couldn't give a stuff what other people think.'

'So what is it?'

For a second Cameron looked as if he was going to say something, then his face closed in. 'Nothing.'

Just then Cloud lifted his grey head and whinnied. Poppy followed his gaze. Three horses were approaching from the direction of Stoney Cross. A palomino led the way, followed by a dark bay and a skewbald.

'Oh no!' cried Scarlett. 'Georgia and her cronies have caught us up.'

FROM THEIR VANTAGE point they watched Georgia and her pony Barley walk up to the gibbet. The showy palomino gelding stood perfectly still as she leant over and reached for the box, stamped her card and read the next clue.

'Who's that with her?' said Poppy.

'Fiona Cavangh-Smythe and Lucy Allerton by the look of it. They were at the Claydon Manor show,' said Sam.

'I remember,' said Poppy. They were the two girls with ringing public school voices who had competed in the same class as her and Scarlett.

'They're at school with Georgia. I think they keep their ponies at Claydon,' said Sam.

Hannah was puzzled. 'Why would they do that?'

'Georgia's parents had to sell most of her jumping ponies and open a livery yard when they spent all their lottery winnings,' said Scarlett, virtually rubbing her hands with glee.

Georgia looked up suddenly, as if she'd heard Scarlett

crowing. She said something to her friends, pointing at their picnic spot.

'Oh no, they've spotted us,' said Scarlett.

'And they're coming over.' Hannah groaned. 'As much as I want to meet the infamous Georgia Canning, I certainly don't want to lose our lead.'

'They might not have guessed the clue,' said Poppy.

'Poppy's right. I don't suppose Georgia knows the moor as well as she and Scarlett do,' said Sam.

Poppy flushed with pleasure. It was true that she and Scarlett knew their corner of Dartmoor as if it was their own back garden, but it was nice of him to say so. An idea that was as delicious as a newly-baked scone popped into her head.

'If they let on that they know the clue is sending us to Witch Cottage, we could say we're taking the short cut through Hickman's Wood so they follow us,' she said.

'But it's in the completely opposite direction,' said Scarlett, her brow crinkling.

'I know that and you know that,' Poppy grinned. 'But does Georgia?'

18

P oppy revealed her cunning plan. 'Once we're in the wood we lose them, double back and head for Princetown and Witch Cottage.'

'Poppy McKeever! You lectured me about hiding the box in the croft at Barrow Tor. Turns out you're as corrupt as I am,' said Hannah admiringly.

'You did what?' spluttered Scott.

'I'm game,' said Sam.

'If you snooze you lose,' agreed Cameron.

'What about you, Scar?' Poppy held her breath. Scarlett had been so cross when Hannah had cheated, she was bound to disagree. But she should have guessed. Moral values were pushed aside when it came to stitching up Georgia Canning.

'It's genius,' she declared. 'Let's do it.'

They raced around collecting the remains of their lunch, tightening girths and pulling down stirrup leathers. By the time Georgia, Fiona and Lucy had reached them they were mounted and ready to go.

Georgia rode Barley alongside Cloud. 'Hi Poppy,' she said. 'How's it going?'

'Good thanks. You?' said Poppy. Although Scarlett disapproved of Georgia, Poppy had never had a problem with her. In fact since the kidnapping they had formed a tentative friendship, exchanging the odd text and occasionally hacking out together, much to Scarlett's annoyance.

'We had a bit of trouble finding the clue at Barrow Tor but other than that good, yeah.'

'Where are the endurance women you were with?' said Scott.

'We went our separate ways after the first clue but I don't think they can be far behind us.'

'What about the others?'

'The team from the riding school near Okehampton have withdrawn because one of their horses pulled up lame. The three boys on cobs are miles off course. They were heading out towards Yelverton the last time we saw them.'

'So it's down to four teams,' said Scott.

'I reckon so,' said Georgia.

'Have you figured out the next clue?' said Poppy.

'Don't tell her, Georgie!' brayed Fiona.

Georgia shot her a scornful look. 'Poppy will have guessed. She knows exactly where the place is. She looked for me there when I was -' Her face clouded over. 'Anyway, there's no way they won't know. Witch Cottage,' she said, jerking her head towards the west.

'That's right,' said Scarlett loudly. 'Only we're taking a short cut, aren't we, guys?'

She turned Red due east and kicked him into a trot. The others nodded vigorously and followed. Scott raised his hand in farewell as Troy crabbed past the three ponies. Poppy tried to ignore the baffled look on Georgia's face as Cloud trotted past, pushing the inevitable pang of guilt aside. It was only a game, she told herself. No-one'll come to any harm. Georgia's used to winning everything she does. It'll do her good to come last for a change. It'll be character-building. In fact, she'd probably end up thanking Poppy.

They kept up a brisk trot until they reached the belt of trees that marked the boundary of Hickman's Wood. It was a strange place: nine acres or so of dwarf oaks whose twisted branches were covered in seaweed-like lichen. Below the oaks' knotted and gnarly boughs, moss-clad boulders were strewn like the pieces of Lego on the floor of Charlie's bedroom.

The wood was a Site of Special Scientific Interest. It was also steeped in myths and folklore.

'Charlie reckons this is the most haunted place on Dartmoor,' Poppy whispered to Hannah, as Cloud and Flynn walked side by side along the ancient Lych Way. 'This path is also known as the Way of the Dead or the Corpse Way because hundreds of years ago it was the route the tenant farmers took when they walked to Lydford to bury their dead.'

Hannah's eyes widened and she gazed around her at the stunted oaks' contorted trunks and branches like arthritic fingers either side of the path. 'It's seriously spooky. I bet the ghosts of highwaymen gallop along here on the night of a full moon.' She shivered. 'OMG, I think I can hear hoofbeats now!'

Poppy felt the hairs on the back of her neck stand up and she flung a look over her shoulder. She breathed a sigh of relief. 'It's only Georgia and the others. They've taken the bait. Now all we need to do is find somewhere to hide.'

Just then the corkscrew-curly branches seemed to grow tighter and the canopy of trees above them heavier. It was as if someone had turned off the overhead light and flicked on a side lamp. Ambient lighting, Poppy thought to herself. It could work to their advantage.

'Scarlett, d'you remember that place we stopped with Charlie?'

Charlie had talked them into riding over to Hickman's Wood the previous summer. He'd cycled alongside them on his mountain bike, but had picked up a puncture halfway through the wood. They'd waited in a hidden corner tucked behind a huge boulder while he mended it. If Poppy remembered correctly the path zigzagged left then right before straightening again. Georgia and her companions would assume they were still a couple of hundred metres ahead until they'd turned the last corner. And by then Poppy and the others would be long gone.

Scarlett's eyes lit up. 'Of course. Follow me!'

19

Scarlett and Red turned sharp right and dropped out of sight behind a boulder as tall as a double decker bus. One by one they followed her, Poppy and Cloud bringing up the rear. Before they plunged into the thicket she glanced behind her. The path was empty. Georgia and her friends had probably decided to leave a healthy distance so Poppy and the others didn't think they were on their tail. Ironically, the decision would be their downfall.

The tiny clearing was just how Poppy remembered. The canopy of branches was so dense and low it was like being in an emerald-green cave. Fitting all six horses in was a squeeze, especially when one was as big as Troy. The iron grey gelding was as solid as a breeze-block wall. He was already pawing the ground and snatching at his bit, impatient to be gone. If he decided to kick off it would be pandemonium.

Cameron rode Floyd alongside Troy and the Welsh cob blew softly into the gelding's nose. He stopped pawing the ground and dropped his head to Floyd's level so he could rub noses with him. Poppy let out the breath she hadn't even realised she'd been holding.

'They've had this bromance going ever since Gran put them in the same paddock,' Sam whispered.

'Just as well. It'd be carnage otherwise,' Poppy whispered back.

'Shush!' screeched Hannah, who was standing up in her stirrups trying to see the path through the tangle of branches. 'That's them!' She held her finger to her lips and they listened to the sound of hoofbeats grow louder and then fainter. Poppy slithered off Cloud, handed his reins to Sam and ducked and weaved her way through the undergrowth towards the path. The rocks were slippery under their coat of moss and once she fell, stifling a yelp as a twinge of pain shot through the ankle she'd sprained the previous year. 'Careful!' she admonished herself. Another sprained ankle was the last thing she needed right now.

Reaching the path she stuck her head out through a gap in the trees and looked left and right. Georgia and the others had gone. The coast was clear. Grinning to herself, she turned back into the trees. As she did she caught a movement out of the corner of her eye. Her breathing quickened and she gripped the stunted trunk of an oak tree and peered along the path. But it was only a squirrel, watching her from the bank opposite with beady eyes as bright as polished onyx.

Poppy raced back to the others.

'They've gone! she said.

'We need to get out of here before they realise they've been tricked,' said Hannah.

Poppy threw herself into the saddle and followed the others out of the clearing. As they cantered back towards Highwayman's Hill she felt a fit of giggles bubbling deep in her belly. Her default position was do everything by the book. She had been a stickler for rules all her life. Yet she had thrown the rulebook out of the window. Georgia and her braying friends would be halfway to Widecombe before they realised they'd been led on a wild goose chase.

Was it cheating or gamesmanship? There was a fine line between the two. But as Poppy crouched over Cloud's neck, his hooves beating their familiar tattoo on the springy moorland grass, she didn't really care. They were on the hunt for a golden horse.

And there were no prizes for coming second.

Poppy hadn't been to Witch Cottage since the previous winter. Then she had ridden over, driven by the conviction that Georgia's captors must be holed up in the tumbledown cottage. She had been wrong, of course. The only inhabitants were a pair of nesting barn owls and a famous wildlife cameraman.

As they emerged from the small band of evergreens that hid the cottage from view Poppy was glad to see it looked the same as always. The front door was still hanging off its hinges, although the winter storms had widened the gaping hole in the catslide roof. The battalion of nettles was back on duty guarding the door.

'Funny isn't it, how this place pulls us back, time and again?' Poppy said to Scarlett as they jumped off their ponies and led them over to the tear-shaped tarn.

Scarlett shivered. 'It's because it's cursed.'

'Cursed?' said Hannah, her interest piqued.

'Too right,' said Scarlett. She launched into the familiar and dubious story of how the croft was haunted by a witch whose son had died in a tin mining accident centuries before.

'She can be seen gliding around the banks of the pool every time there's a full moon,' she told Hannah.

'Have you seen her?'

'D'you think I'd be stupid enough to come up here in the middle of the night? No thank you. I leave that kind of stuff to Poppy. Anyway, it's all true. My Granny Martha told me.'

'Don't believe a word of it,' said Poppy.

Scarlett shrugged and handed her the card. 'You can fight the nettles and go and find the box then.'

'Be an angel and do ours, too?' said Scott with a lazy smile.

Poppy tutted, looped Cloud's reins over the old fence post she always used and, dodging Troy's enormous hooves, reached up for Scott's card.

'Now to do battle with the nettles,' she muttered. But as she neared the door she realised someone had already stamped a path through them. Did that mean the endurance riders had somehow passed them and were now in the lead? It was possible, but unlikely. It couldn't be Georgia and her friends - they could never have overtaken them, even if they'd realised they were heading in the opposite direction. No, it must have been whoever was planting the clues.

Keeping to the trail of broken nettle stems, Poppy eased the door open, hoping its rusty hinges didn't choose that moment to give way, and stepped inside. The air smelt as fusty as it had the first time she'd explored the old shepherd's croft and, as she crossed the quarry floor tiles in the parlour, she was transported back to the previous summer, when she'd discovered Caitlin's diary and found a stash of stolen phones in the tiny loft.

Which was where the next clue was, according to the riddle. Poppy opened the door into the kitchen and was about to run up the narrow staircase when she heard the unmistakable sound of a floorboard creaking. At first she assumed it was her. Until she remembered the whole of the downstairs of Witch Cottage was tiled with quarry tiles. And though they might have been cracked and crumbling, quarry tiles didn't creak. She froze, the hairs on the back of her neck standing to attention, and glanced upwards. As she did the floorboard creaked again, sending a shower of dust right into her eyes.

'Ow!' she cried, scrunching her eyes closed. She fought an instinct to rub them fiercely with her fists, but blinked instead, hoping her tears would wash the dust away.

She was still blinking madly as the sound of heavy footsteps trudged across the floor above her and clumped down the stairs. Poppy forced her eyes open and took a step back as a figure swam into focus in front of her.

20

T
he heavy footsteps belonged to a man with hooded eyes and greying hair as short as a soldier's. Although hardly taller than Poppy, he nevertheless looked as wiry as a terrier with sinewy arms and brawny shoulders. He also looked familiar, although she couldn't place him.

'You found the place then?' he said in an Irish accent.

Poppy took another step back, her hands finding the edge of the range. His brogue wasn't soft and melodic like Cameron's. It was guttural and rough, his words sounding more like a threat than a question.

Poppy swallowed. 'Yes,' she said faintly, glancing up. 'It's in the loft.'

The man nodded and spat into a dark corner of the tiny kitchen. If he noticed Poppy flinch, he didn't show it. He ran a hand over his close-cropped hair with nicotine-stained fingers. That was when Poppy remembered where she had seen him before. He'd been at Eaglestone Arabians the day they'd visited. He was the man who'd led Eddie Eaglestone's famous stallion Fearless Flight into the yard. He was the stud's head groom. Poppy fished around in her memory for his name. Micky Murphy. That was it. Eddie Eaglestone's right hand man. He must be helping run the treasure hunt and was here setting the clue. She exhaled slowly.

'Well, go on then,' he barked, gesturing at the stairs.

Poppy raced lightly up the stairs two at a time, her heart thudding in her chest. A wooden crate had been left under the open loft hatch and she stood on it and reached into the loft. She worked her way around the hatch, sighing with relief when her hand came to rest on a small square box. She lifted it down and stamped the fourth square on each card with an orange dancing horse. There were only two empty squares left.

She was walking over to the window so she had enough light to read the clue when she heard another creak. Micky Murphy was at the top of the stairs watching her.

'Finished?' he said.

'Almost.' Poppy peered blearily into the box and read and re-read the clue until she was happy she had memorised it. 'There,' she said, handing it back to him.

The head groom's pale blue eyes bored a hole in her and she hopped from foot to foot, a sense of unease making her fidgety. Although she had never believed a word of Scarlett's dire warnings about Witch Cottage she had a sudden urge to put a long distance between her and the old croft.

'I'll be off then,' she muttered, backing out of the bedroom, down the stairs and out of the door before Micky Murphy could say another word.

The air outside smelt clean and fresh and she breathed in deep lungfuls of it. She bounded over to Cloud and threw her arms around his neck as if she hadn't seen him for weeks. He nuzzled her pocket and she found a couple of stray pony nuts and gave them to him. He whickered with pleasure.

'OK?' said Sam, riding Star close. 'You look a bit pale.'

Back outside, with the warmth of the sun on her face and her friends around her, she wondered why she had felt so jumpy. She flashed Sam a smile and sprang into the saddle.

'Nah, I'm fine.'

'Have you got the clue?' said Hannah.

Poppy tapped her forehead. 'It's all in here, don't worry. I'll tell you on the way.'

BY THE TIME they clip-clopped up the drive of Eaglestone Arabians an hour and a half later Poppy was exhausted. Six hours in the saddle had taken its toll and her back was stiff and her legs sore. Hannah, used to an hour's lesson once a week back in Teddington, was complaining bitterly to anyone within earshot that her backside had gone completely numb. Cloud and Red, both so fizzy when they'd set off, were walking sedately side by side, their necks stretched and their ears pricked. Flynn plodded behind them, as weary as his rider. Even Troy was loping along as calmly as a ladies' hack. They would all sleep well tonight, Poppy decided with a rueful smile.

A young groom pushing a wheelbarrow towards an immaculate muck heap saw them and stopped.

'The campsite's over there,' she said, pointing to a small paddock to the right of the yard. 'The tents are to go in there and you're to turn your horses out in the field behind it.'

'Where are the facilities?' said Hannah.

The girl pushed a length of blonde hair out of her eyes and picked up the handles of the wheelbarrow. 'In the corner,' she said with a jerk of her head.

'Great. A Portaloo,' Scarlett grumbled.

'It's an adventure,' Poppy reminded her two friends.

She jumped off Cloud and led him through the gate into

the field. 'Do you think they'll be alright, all in together?' she said, eyeing Troy dubiously.

'They'll be grand. They're all so tired they'll just want to eat and rest,' said Cameron.

Unconvinced, Poppy whispered in Cloud's ear, 'Keep away from that nutter,' as she slid his bridle over his ears. He walked away with a swish of his tail and grunted with pleasure as he sank to his knees and rolled. His hooves waved in the air as he rubbed his neck and then staggered to his feet and gave a shake, leaving a smattering of white hairs like a memory in the short spring grass.

Caroline had left their tent and supplies in a small field shelter and once Poppy was happy Cloud was settled she began lugging the tent over to one of two fire pits in the middle of the paddock.

'Which way's west?' she wondered aloud.

Sam, who was pulling a small green inflatable tent out of its bag, looked at the sun. 'That way,' he said. 'Why?'

'Charlie said to make sure the tent's not facing west because of the prevailing wind. In case it rains,' she added.

'So you *were* listening to him,' teased Hannah.

Poppy grinned. 'Promise you won't tell?'

Hannah placed her hand on her heart. 'I promise,' she said solemnly.

They spent the next half an hour pushing the tent poles through the flaps in the nylon, just as Charlie had shown them. Once the two poles were in position they tightened the guy ropes and hammered in the tent pegs. Poppy threw the fly sheet over the top of the tent and Scarlett and Hannah fastened it to the ground.

'Make sure you leave a gap,' Poppy reminded them.

'Alright bossy boots,' said Scarlett.

Scarlett and Hannah rolled out the camping mats and sleeping bags while Poppy sorted through their provisions.

They'd packed sausages, baked beans and rolls, with bacon and more rolls for the morning. Caroline, who was an old hand at camping, had frozen the sausages and bacon to stop it spoiling. She had also found them a small camping stove in Waterby Post Office and Stores. Poppy gave the sausages a squeeze, wondering what they would eat if they hadn't defrosted. But she needn't have worried. They were cold but squidgy. Her stomach rumbled.

'Is it too early to eat?' she called to the others.

'Absolutely not. I'm ravenous,' said Scarlett, peering into Sam's cold box. 'Yum. Quiche, coleslaw and potato salad. And chocolate cake. Sam's mum is a brilliant cook,' she told Hannah.

'And I'm not. So she said she'd make us stuff that didn't need cooking,' said Sam.

'Caroline's packed flapjacks and strawberries. If we share everything we'll have a real feast,' said Poppy.

Sam's eyes crinkled. 'It's a deal.'

Hannah flopped down beside them. 'Where are Scott and Cameron?'

'Scott's gone on his date. The last time I saw Cameron he was heading towards the yard.'

Poppy frowned. 'I thought it was out of bounds.' The directive in the small print had been clear: *Access to the yard and house is prohibited at all times and under any circumstance.* It had seemed a bit draconian, but it hadn't stopped Poppy signing.

'Well, that's where he's gone.'

'No sign of the others,' said Scarlett, pricking sausages with a fork and arranging them in her brother's small frying pan.

'That's good. Means we're still in the lead,' said Sam.

Hannah shook her head. 'Not really. We're no better off than the rest of them if we're all setting off at the same time tomorrow. Makes today a bit pointless if you think about it.'

'I don't suppose Eddie Eaglestone did think about it. He doesn't strike me as someone who's organised many treasure hunts in his time,' said Scarlett.

'The other teams might not have all four clues yet,' Poppy pointed out. 'We only have two more to go, remember.'

'Speaking of which, are you actually going to tell us the next one?' said Scarlett.

'Yeah, tell us now before the others arrive,' said Hannah.

Poppy held up her hand. 'OK, just let me remember it.' She pictured the musty cottage, the wooden box and the clue she'd read over and over, trying to ignore the memory of Micky Murphy's hooded eyes boring into her.

'Oh no, you haven't forgotten it, have you?' said Scarlett. She turned to Hannah and Sam. 'She's only gone and forgotten it. What are we going to do now?'

21

'Shush!' Poppy cried. Her mind had gone completely blank, just like it had the day of the show at Claydon, when she had completely forgotten the course the minute she was about to ride into the ring.

'For goodness sake, just be quiet so I can remember.' She closed her eyes. It was something about fish. If she could remember the first line the rest would follow, she was sure of it.

'Name some types of fish!' she said.

Three pairs of eyebrows shot up.

'Fish?' said Sam uncertainly.

'Fish,' Poppy confirmed.

'Cod,' said Hannah.

Poppy shook her head.

'Goldfish,' said Scarlett.

Poppy gave her a withering look.

'Tuna!' yelled Hannah.

'Smoked mackerel!' shouted Scarlett.

'Plaice?' said Sam.

Poppy shook her head. 'Keep going.'

'Sardines!'

'Lobster!'

'Lobster's not a fish, you idiot.'

'Trout?' said Sam.

Poppy touched her nose with one index finger and pointed to Sam with the other. 'Not quite. What's the fish that's a bit like trout but bigger?'

'Salmon!' the other three chorused.

Poppy nodded and her face split into a grin. Salmon, that was it. Of course. She took a deep breath and recited the riddle.

> *'Salmons leap*
> *The wild ones swim*
> *Above I am still*
> *Below, full of vim.'*

She looked at them expectantly. 'So, any ideas?'

'It's a river,' said Hannah decisively.

'Oh yes, that narrows it down a bit. Because there aren't many rivers on Dartmoor,' said Scarlett, her voice heavy with sarcasm.

'Alright clever clogs, tell us what you think.'

'What does it mean, the wild ones?' Scarlett said.

'It's a book, isn't it?' said Poppy.

'You're thinking of *Where the Wild Things Are*,' said Sam. His face reddened. 'Mum used to read it to me when I was little.'

'Do you think it's a waterfall?' said Hannah suddenly. 'Because the water is still at the top and full of vim below?'

They all considered this.

'Maybe,' said Scarlett.

'Definitely,' said Sam.

'Or a weir,' said Poppy, jumping to her feet. 'There's one

at Combe Falls. We went one autumn a couple of years ago to watch the salmon leaping upstream to spawn.' Charlie had taken his camera, keen to capture the slivers of silver as the fish leapt heroically up the sheer face of the weir. 'There's a viewing platform,' Poppy remembered. 'And a lifebuoy because it's popular with wild swimmers -'

'The wild ones!' said Hannah.

'Combe Falls it is. Good job, Poppy,' said Sam. 'How far is it from here?'

'It's back over towards Hickman's Wood. It shouldn't take much more than an hour.' Poppy was about to sit back down when she heard the unmistakable sound of metal shoe on tarmac. She stood on tiptoes and squinted into the sun. Three horses were trotting briskly up the drive, as perky as if they'd only just set off. It was the endurance riders on their Arab horses.

'Still no sign of Canning and her cronies,' Scarlett crowed.

'Don't,' said Poppy, who couldn't shake off the feeling of guilt weighing heavily in the pit of her stomach.

'Remember, not a word about the clue,' warned Hannah.

They nodded to the three women and watched as they led their horses into the paddock and expertly made their tent by the second fire pit.

The sausages were beginning to spit in the pan when Georgia, Fiona and Lucy arrived on sweaty-looking ponies.

'Uh oh,' said Poppy, hoping the ground would swallow her up.

'Perhaps they didn't even realise it was a trick,' said Hannah.

But she was wrong. Georgia jumped off Barley, flung his reins at Lucy and marched over.

'I suppose you think you're funny,' she said, addressing Scarlett.

'I don't know what you're talking about,' said Scarlett, winking at the others.

'Don't give me that. You deliberately tried to sabotage our chances.'

'Oh, take a chill pill,' said Scarlett. 'It's only a bit of fun.'

'Fun?' said Georgia. 'Luckily we realised what you'd done and made it to Witch Cottage, but no thanks to you. Well, here's a word of advice. I'd watch your backs from now on if I were you.'

Scarlett stepped forward. 'Are you threatening us?'

Georgia's icy blue eyes flashed dangerously. 'It's not a threat. It's a promise.'

Poppy felt sick. It had been her idea yet Georgia was laying the blame firmly at Scarlett's jodhpur boot-clad feet.

'Sorry Georgia. We thought everyone would be playing tricks. All's fair in love, war and treasure hunts,' she finished lamely.

'Oh, it's OK Poppy. I know you weren't to blame. You would never stoop so low.' She glared at Scarlett. 'You should know me well enough by now that this'll just make me more determined to win. That golden horse is in the bag.' With that she turned on her heels and stalked back to Fiona, Lucy and the three ponies.

Poppy watched miserably as Georgia and the others set up their tent next to the endurance riders. She hated confrontation of any kind and to think she was the root cause of such an unpleasant clash made her squirm with shame.

Scarlett and Hannah were unperturbed.

'She'll get over it,' shrugged Scarlett.

'Worse things happen at sea,' agreed Hannah.

'Oh look, there's Cameron,' said Sam with relief.

Cameron strode past them to the field shelter and

rummaged around in his rucksack, appearing a few seconds later.

'Have any of you been in my bag?'

'Of course not,' said Poppy.

'Why, is something missing?' said Hannah.

Cameron ran a hand through his hair. 'No,' he said eventually. 'It just looks different.'

Poppy handed him a plate of food. 'What were you doing?' she said.

Cameron glanced at the block of stables and smiled thinly. 'I was doing what we're all doing, Poppy. I was looking for the golden horse.'

22

When the sun dipped below the horizon Sam lit the kindling in the fire pit and they sat with their sleeping bags around their shoulders, toasted marshmallows on the end of kebab sticks and talked.

'What do you all want to do when you leave school?' said Poppy.

'I want to go to art school to study fashion design,' said Hannah. Poppy nodded. She could picture Hannah working in fashion. 'What about you, Sam?' she said, realising that because they went to different schools she had no idea what subjects he liked, let alone what career he wanted.

'I'm going to be a vet. Specialising in horses, of course,' he said.

Scarlett's mouth formed a perfect circle. 'But you have to be super brainy for that!'

Sam gave an embarrassed laugh. 'I'm pretty good at science. It should be fine.'

'What about you, Scarlett O'Hara?' said Hannah.

'I'm going to stay and work on the farm.'

Poppy stared at her best friend. 'I didn't know you wanted to do that.'

'What did you think I wanted to do?'

'I don't know. Go to uni with me, I suppose.'

'I'll probably go to agricultural college, but there's no way I'm going to uni. And I'm not leaving the farm. Alex has already said he's off to London as soon as he's old enough, and Mum and Dad'll need some help.'

'Oh.' Poppy tried not to feel deflated. They spent so much time together Caroline sometimes joked they were tied at the hip. Poppy had assumed that if she went to university, Scarlett would come, too.

'What about you, Cameron?' she asked, hoping no-one had noticed her discomfiture. She didn't really expect him to answer. He was normally so reserved. But to her surprise he leant forward, his green eyes fervent.

'I'm going to do what my old man never had the chance to do. I'm going to breed Arabians.'

'Ah, is that why you're here - so you can pinch a few ideas from Eddie Eaglestone?' asked Scarlett, elbowing him in the ribs.

He rubbed his chin. 'Something like that.'

'Anyway, what do *you* want to do, Poppy?' said Hannah.

They all turned to look at her, their faces lit by the flames dancing in the fire pit.

Poppy shrugged. 'I have absolutely no idea.'

WHEN THE FIRE had burned down to a few smouldering embers they decided to turn in for the night. Poppy picked up their torch and walked across the dewy grass to say goodnight to Cloud. He was snoozing next to Red close to the gate, his near hindleg resting and his head low.

'Hey baby,' Poppy crooned and he opened an eye and whickered. She pulled up a couple of handfuls of grass and held out her palm, smiling as his whiskers tickled her wrist. She ran her hand down his legs checking for heat and, satisfied there wasn't any, scratched the soft spot beneath his right ear until he gave a contented sigh. Star wandered over to say hello and she rubbed the black mare's forehead. She scanned the field for Flynn. Normally the greedy Dartmoor would be the first to come over looking for treats but he was nowhere to be seen. Poppy shone the torch from left to right, keeping the beam low so she didn't blind the horses. Troy and Floyd were standing nose to tail to the right. Beyond them the three Arabs, Barley and Fiona and Lucy's ponies were grazing in the moonlight.

'Where is he?' she muttered, working back across the field until the beam fell on a dark bay Flynn-sized shape lying flat in the grass.

Poppy's heart gave a flip. Training the torch beam on him, she gave a low whistle. He didn't move. A wave of panic washed over her. He was alright, wasn't he? Dartmoor ponies were known for their stamina, but at fifteen he was much older than the others. He was also far less fit. Her mouth dry, she darted across the field, skidding to a halt a couple of metres away from him.

'Flynn,' she called softly, watching his flanks carefully. Were they moving? It was impossible to tell. 'Flynn,' she called again, louder this time. She held a hand out and touched his rump tentatively. It was warm. 'Flynn,' she called for a third time.

The little bay gelding's head shot up and he staggered to his feet, spinning around to face her. Poppy's hand flew to her mouth. 'Oh Flynn. I didn't mean to scare you!'

He eyed her warily, his nostrils flared. 'It's only me,' she said. 'Poppy,' she added, in case he hadn't worked it out.

Flynn gave a little shake of his head, as if he'd suddenly clocked that the creature that had pulled him from his deep slumber was indeed Poppy and not some marauding mountain lion intent on supper. He bustled over to her and nudged her crossly.

'I'm sorry,' said Poppy, digging deep in her pocket for the last remaining Polos she'd been saving for Cloud. 'You have them,' she told him, thumbing them onto her hand and feeding them to him one by one.

Apparently mollified, he lifted his head and nuzzled Poppy's neck. 'I really am sorry,' she said. With a flick of his tail he lowered his head and began tearing mouthfuls of grass. Poppy watched him until her heart rate had returned to normal. She stifled a yawn and clumped back across the field.

Then a bloodcurdling scream pierced the air, followed by an ear-splitting shriek, stopping Poppy in her tracks.

23

The noise was coming from their tent. Poppy quickened her pace, remembering the murderous look Georgia had given Scarlett earlier. She arrived to find a worried-looking Sam and Cameron outside.

'What on earth -?' The question died on her lips as another screech, as loud as a barn owl, rang out.

'Take that, Scarlett O'Hara!'

'Not so fast, city girl!'

A muffled yelp was followed by peals of laughter. Poppy stepped forward and unzipped the tent. Scarlett and Hannah, each clutching a pillow, stared guiltily at her. From across the field, one of the endurance riders yelled at them to kill the noise.

'Oops,' giggled Hannah, putting her finger to her lips.

'It was only a pillow fight,' said Scarlett, blowing her fringe out of her eyes.

'It sounded as if someone was being murdered in their bed,' said Poppy reasonably. She rolled her eyes at Cameron and Sam. 'Don't worry, I'll keep an eye on them. You'd better get some sleep.'

Muttering goodnights, the boys disappeared back into their own tent. Poppy ducked into theirs. 'I suppose I'd better go in the middle to stop you two fighting,' she said.

'Piggy in the middle!' cried Scarlett and Hannah, convulsing with laughter.

Poppy tutted. 'Actually, I was thinking more a rose between two thorns.'

If Poppy had thought sleep would be impossible sandwiched between her two friends like a trio of over-friendly penguins she was wrong. She fell into a deep and dreamless slumber the moment her head touched the pillow. It seemed just seconds later that Hannah woke her with a gentle shake. She groaned and pulled her sleeping bag over her head.

'Five more minutes,' she muttered.

Hannah began unzipping her sleeping bag.

'Go away!'

'Not a chance. Come on, Poppy, wake up! Georgia and the endurance women have already gone. We need to get going!'

Poppy lifted her head off the pillow and scowled at Hannah. Beside her, Scarlett's sleeping bag was empty.

'Where's Scar?'

'Cooking breakfast.'

As if on cue, the smell of bacon wafted into the open tent. Poppy realised she was ravenous. She reached for her jodhpurs.

'What time is it anyway?' she grumbled.

'Half past eight! The boys have already packed their tent away. They promised to give us a hand if we cooked them breakfast. So you need to get up. Now!'

'OK! I heard you the first time.'

As she emerged from the tent Scarlett handed her a bacon

butty and a carton of orange juice and she sat crosslegged next to Sam.

'Alright Sleeping Beauty?' he grinned.

She elbowed him in the ribs. 'Ha ha, very funny.' She took a bite of the butty and a dribble of bacon fat ran down her chin. She wiped it off with the back of her hand, hoping Sam hadn't noticed. 'What time did the others leave?'

'We woke up just before eight and they'd already gone.' He pointed to his own chin. 'You've missed a bit.'

Poppy reddened and gave her chin another wipe. They chewed in companionable silence as Scarlett pottered about in their makeshift outdoor kitchen and Cameron helped Hannah roll up their sleeping bags and mats. Poppy was taking a final swig of orange juice when the birdsong was interrupted by the guttural roar of a motorbike.

'Scott's back,' said Scarlett, wiping her hands on her jods and smoothing down her unruly curls. They watched the black and silver bike snake up the drive and come to a stop by the field gate. Scott hung his helmet on the handlebar, peeled off his leathers to reveal a denim blue teeshirt and jodhpurs underneath and sauntered over.

'All ready for day two of our exciting treasure hunt?' He gave them a lazy grin.

'I guess,' said Sam. 'How was your hot date?'

'So so,' said Scott. 'She wasn't really my cup of tea. Speaking of which…'

Scarlett stepped forward, her hands wrapped around a tin mug of steaming builders' tea. 'Strong and sweet, just how you like it,' she trilled.

'You're a doll,' said Scott, taking a gulp.

'We didn't get offered tea,' groused Poppy.

'Well, I don't have time to make you one now. We need to be out of here in fifteen minutes.' Scarlett stood with her hands on her hips. 'Hannah and Cameron can pack the tent,

I'll sort the rest of it out. You and Sam catch the horses. And Scott,' she smiled sweetly at him. 'Can you get the tack? It's in the field shelter.'

One by one Poppy and Sam caught the horses and tied them up.

'We only have time to flick a brush over them and pick out their feet,' said Sam.

Poppy gazed disconsolately at the grass stains that spread up Cloud's hindquarters like green mould on a damp bathroom wall.

'How come you're so filthy yet Troy the nutter horse has managed to stay beautifully clean?' she scolded him, picking up a body brush. She cast an envious look at Star, whose black coat shone like molasses.

'You're so lucky having a black pony,' she told Sam. Then Cloud bent his head to nuzzle her back as she brushed his foreleg and she felt a stab of reproach. What a stupid thing to say. She was lucky to have a pony at all, let alone a superstar pony who would risk his life for her in a heartbeat. She dropped the brush and flung her arms around his neck, burying her face in his mane. 'I don't mean it,' she said thickly. 'Who cares about grass stains? Green is the new grey, anyway.'

'Sorry to interrupt your little love-in,' drawled Scott's voice behind her. 'But where did you say you'd left the tack?'

Poppy bent down to pick up the brush. 'In the field shelter.'

'Well, it's not there now,' said Scott.

'Haha, very funny.'

'I'm not joking, Poppy. There's no tack in the field shelter. It's gone.'

24

'But it was right here!' Poppy pointed to the far corner of the field shelter, Cloud's body brush still in her hand. She gazed around her with mounting panic. Two sets of camping equipment were stacked neatly in one corner, waiting to be picked up later. But the corner they'd bagged, and where they'd so carefully stored their saddles and bridles, was empty bar a bale of hay and an upturned bucket with a broken handle.

'I'm calling the police,' said Scott grimly, reaching for his phone. 'Six sets of tack is worth thousands.'

'Wait,' said Poppy. 'We should double check the others haven't taken it first.'

But it was clear the minute Poppy asked them that they hadn't been anywhere near the tack. They raced over to the field shelter and stared helplessly at the empty corner.

The colour leached from Scarlett's face, making her freckles more pronounced than ever.

'I saved my wages for months to buy Red's saddle,' she wailed.

'Don't worry, we'll find it,' said Poppy with more conviction than she felt.

'Surely we'd have heard someone taking it last night? They'd have needed a vehicle to cart it all away,' said Sam.

'How did anyone even know it was here?' cried Hannah.

A muscle was twitching in Cameron's jaw. 'I should have known something like this would happen,' he said, giving the bucket a vicious kick.

All eyes swivelled in his direction.

'What do you mean?' said Poppy slowly. It occurred to her that they knew nothing about the enigmatic Irish boy other than the little he'd told them. Could he have...*would* he have...?

'Wait - what's that?' said Hannah, picking up a folded piece of paper that had been concealed by the bucket. Her eyes widened and then narrowed. She thrust the paper into Poppy's hand.

Poppy scanned the hastily-scrawled note and shook her head. She should have known their trick would backfire.

'What does it say!' said Scarlett, jumping from foot to foot.

Poppy cleared her throat and read.

> *'Can you win with no tack?*
> *Your chances are low*
> *Don't prank a prankster*
> *You reap what you sow.'*

'Georgia!' cried Scarlett.

'You don't think it's Eaglestone, playing some twisted game with us?' said Cameron.

Poppy gave him an incredulous look. 'Why on earth would he do that? Of course it's Georgia, paying us back for yesterday. And it's all my fault. If we'd played fair and square none of this would have happened,' she added flatly.

'We might as well pull out now. There's no way we can ride without saddles and bridles,' said Hannah.

Scott shrugged. 'I'm game to give it a try.'

'Me too,' said Cameron.

'Well, I'm not,' said Hannah.

'Let's not make any rash decisions,' said Sam. 'I don't suppose they managed to take the tack very far, do you? I reckon they've hidden it somewhere. We just need to work out where.'

'Sam's right,' said Poppy. 'It's a prank, she says as much in her note.'

Scarlett nodded. 'OK, so let's split up and start looking. Scott and I will check the two fields. Hannah, you and Sam look along the driveway. And Poppy and Cameron can search the yard.'

'The bit that's out of bounds? Great,' said Poppy sarcastically.

'The tack wouldn't be missing if it wasn't for you, remember,' Hannah pointed out.

'Would you two please stop ganging up on me?' Poppy said hotly. She turned to Cameron. 'Come on, we've obviously drawn the short straw. We'd better do as we're told.'

They crossed the field past the Portaloo towards the stables. Poppy paused and glanced back at the plastic cubicle.

'They wouldn't, would they?' she wondered aloud.

Cameron pulled a face. 'I hope not.'

Poppy pinched her nose and pulled open the door with the tips of her fingers. 'No, they wouldn't,' she said with relief, letting the door slam shut. 'So where are we going to look first?'

Cameron was walking so fast Poppy had to run to catch up.

'You know how people talk about hiding things in plain sight?' he said.

'Not really,' she puffed. 'What does it mean?'

'Keeping things in such an obvious place that people don't notice them.'

'So where would you hide six sets of tack?' said Poppy. And then she hit her forehead with the heel of her hand. 'The tack room!' she cried.

Cameron nodded. 'We'll look there first.'

'But we don't know where it is.'

Cameron flashed her a smile. 'I do. Just stay close and if anyone asks what we're doing tell them the truth. That another team has hidden our tack.'

Poppy didn't have time to wonder how Cameron knew where Eddie Eaglestone's tack room was, because he disappeared through a narrow gap in the stables. She plunged into the gap after him and they emerged in the centre of the yard. It was as pristine as it had been on the open day. The exquisitely chiselled heads of a dozen Arab horses watched them over their stable doors.

'Which one's Fearless Flight?' Poppy whispered.

Cameron pointed to a loose box at the far end of the line of stables opposite them. The stallion tossed his head, his flaxen mane rippling like a river of molten gold. He really was stunning.

Cameron gave Poppy a tight smile. 'Want to go and say hello?'

'We don't have time, do we?'

'Ah, it won't take a minute.' Cameron looked left and right but there was no-one around. He sauntered across the perfect grass to Flight's loose box.

'Hey boy,' he said softly. The stallion lowered his head and nuzzled Cameron's pocket. Cameron pulled out a half-opened packet of Polos and offered him a couple, which he snatched greedily.

Something about the horse was perplexing Poppy, making the hairs on the back of her neck stand up. Sure, it was the first time she'd ever been so close to a stallion and his sheer presence was breathtaking. She could sense the phenomenal energy coming off him in waves. But it wasn't that. Yes, he looked familiar, but that was because she'd seen him at the open day. No, it was the way he was so at ease with Cameron. And he had zoomed in on the Irish boy's pocket as if he knew the Polos were there.

'He recognises you!' she said.

Cameron threw a nervous look over his shoulder, but they were still alone.

Poppy's imagination began working overtime. Cameron had come such a long way to visit a stud. Why? They weren't exactly short of them back home in Ireland, after all. He had sneaked off to the yard the previous evening, even though it was out of bounds. What for? He was obviously obsessed with Arab horses - why else would he carry the picture of an Arabian colt around with him? And he knew exactly which stable Eddie Eaglestone kept his priceless stallion in. Suddenly everything clicked into place.

'Oh my God, you're going to take him, aren't you?'

25

Cameron gave her a bemused stare. 'What are you talking about?'

'Taking part in the treasure hunt is just a front. You're here to steal Fearless Flight. It's obvious.'

Cameron gave a short bark of laughter. '*I'm* going to steal *him*?' he scoffed. 'If only you knew.'

But Poppy wasn't listening. She was too caught up in the heat of her hypothesis. 'I bet there's a black market for horses like him, especially in the Middle East. All those rich Sheiks with their billions. How much are you getting?' Her eyes widened. 'And now I've worked it out I'll be an accessory!'

Cameron ran his hands through his hair. 'Shut up, Poppy,' he said. 'You don't know what you're talking about.'

'Oh, but I do,' Poppy said self-righteously. 'And I'm going to tell Eddie Eaglestone exactly what you're up to. Stealing horses is not OK, Cameron. And I can't - I *won't* - let you get away with it.'

As Poppy turned for the farmhouse Cameron lunged after her, grabbing her arm.

'No!' he cried.

Poppy tried to twist away but his grip on her arm was as tight as a tourniquet.

'You're hurting me! Let me go!' she cried.

A clatter of buckets at the far end of the yard made them both jump and Cameron dropped Poppy's arm as if he'd been scorched. His face turned pale as Micky Murphy marched over.

'Listen,' he hissed out of the corner of his mouth. 'I'll tell you everything, OK? Why I'm here. Why I carry that picture around. Why I'm so interested in Fearless Flight. Just don't tell him who I am or what you think I'm going to do. Because you are wrong, Poppy,' he said hoarsely. 'You are so very wrong.'

Poppy rubbed her arm and looked sidelong at Cameron. The raw emotion in his voice had sowed a seed of doubt in her mind.

'You'll tell me everything?' she said.

He nodded. 'Everything.'

'No lies?'

'The truth, the whole truth and nothing but the truth,' he said, placing his hand on his heart.

Poppy jerked her head towards Micky Murphy, who was bearing down on them like a human tsunami.

'So what do we tell him?'

'That we're looking for our tack, remember.'

Their tack. Of course. Poppy had forgotten all about it. She gave a tiny nod and wondered, as Cameron exhaled slowly, if she would live to regret her decision.

Murphy stood in front of them with his arms folded. His forearms were as muscular as a boxer's and were covered in faded tattoos. His eyes narrowed as he recognised Poppy.

'You again! What the hell do you think you're doing? You've been told the yard is out of bounds.'

Poppy licked her lips and glanced at Cameron. He was

staring defiantly at the older man, a challenge in his eyes. In that moment he reminded her of someone, but as she tried to order her thoughts Murphy took another step forward and growled, 'Well?'

Fearless Flight snorted and retreated to the back of his stable.

Poppy took a deep breath. 'We were just…um, you know, um…looking for -'

'What Poppy is trying to say,' Cameron interjected smoothly, 'is that we were looking for our tack.'

Poppy gaped at him open-mouthed. Because all traces of his lilting Irish accent had completely vanished. He sounded as West Country as the rest of them.

'Your tack?'

'Our tack,' Cameron repeated sadly. 'I'm afraid one of the other teams played a prank on us and hid it. All six sets! We came over to see if it had been left in the tack room but were sidetracked by Fearless Flight.'

'He's so beautiful we just had to come and say hello,' said Poppy, finally finding her voice. 'We're very sorry. We didn't realise it was a problem.'

Micky Murphy unfolded his arms and reached for the phone in his back pocket. Poppy held her breath. Was he about to call the police and have them arrested for plotting a theft? Was that even a crime? No. Conspiracy to steal - that's what they called it. But Poppy hadn't conspired to do anything. She had just followed Cameron straight into the lion's den.

'Mags, it's me,' Micky Murphy growled into his phone.

Poppy felt her stomach muscles unclench just a fraction.

'I've got two kids from the treasure hunt looking for their tack. See if it's in the tack room, will you? No, I'll hold.'

He held the phone away from his ear. 'You two wait here where I can keep an eye on you.'

After a few minutes the silence was broken by a tinny voice emanating from the handset. Murphy listened and nodded.

'We'll be right over.' He ended the call and turned his attention back to Poppy and Cameron. 'Seems like you were right. Your tack's in the tack room.'

Cameron glanced into Flight's stable before smiling knowingly at the head groom. 'Hidden in plain sight,' he said. 'I had a feeling it would be.'

POPPY HOOKED Cloud's bridle over one shoulder and balanced his saddle on her arm under the watchful eye of the blonde groom who'd directed them to their campsite the previous evening. She followed Cameron out of the tack room and back through the gap in the stables to the paddock beyond.

Once she was sure they were out of earshot she said, 'Since when did you speak with a Devon accent?'

Cameron was carrying two saddles, one on each arm. Tension was etched in pen and ink lines across his forehead. 'Since now,' he replied shortly.

'But why?'

'Not now, Poppy.'

'You promised you'd tell me what's going on!'

He sighed. 'And I will. Let's get out of here first. I'll tell you on the way to Combe Falls, OK?'

Poppy swapped Cloud's saddle to her other arm. 'I suppose it'll have to be.'

26

Twenty minutes later they were ready to go. Scott and Sam led the way back down the drive.

'We've got so much time to catch up thanks to Georgia Flippin' Canning,' grumbled Scarlett.

'If she wins, I'm calling for a steward's enquiry,' said Hannah, guiding Flynn next to Red. Red flattened his ears and snaked his neck at the sturdy Dartmoor pony but Poppy knew it was all show. They got on like a house on fire when no-one was watching. A bit like Scarlett and Hannah, come to mention it.

With her friends' attention fully engaged in a joint rant about Georgia, Poppy seized the chance to ride alongside Cameron. Floyd was a hand bigger than Cloud but the two geldings matched each other stride for stride.

'He's a nice stamp of a pony,' Cameron said, nodding at Cloud.

Poppy ran her hand along Cloud's neck. 'He is.'

'Have you ever seen the Connemaras running wild on the west coast of Ireland?'

Poppy shook her head. 'Have you?'

'My dad took me once, when I was a lad. But I still remember like it was yesterday. Greys and blacks and browns running like wild mustangs across the peat bogs and fields of clover. They were brave and beautiful. Full of spirit, y'know?'

Poppy did know. Cameron's description suited Cloud perfectly.

'Some say they're descended from Arabian horses,' he said.

'I didn't know that.'

'That's what my dad told me, anyway. When ships from the Spanish Armada sank off the west coast of Ireland in 1588 their horses swam ashore and bred with the native ponies. I suppose that's why he liked them so much. They reminded him of Arabs.'

This passion for Arab horses, Poppy mused. Was this what linked Cameron and his dad to Eddie Eaglestone? Was it a shared love of the breed that had driven Cameron to cross the Irish Sea in search of a famous Arabian stallion?

'Your dad loves Arabs?' Poppy ventured.

'He did. Not any more. He's dead,' said Cameron flatly. 'He died last week.'

'Oh,' cried Poppy. 'I'm sorry. I didn't realise.'

A shadow crossed Cameron's face. 'Why should you?'

'You seem very -' Poppy paused. She didn't want him to take it the wrong way. 'You seem very *together* about it all.'

'He and Mum broke up when I was ten. It wasn't exactly an amicable split. We moved back to Dublin and he was always away touring. I hadn't seen him for years. I've been used to not having him around.'

Poppy digested this. 'What do you mean, he was away touring?'

'He had a band. You've probably never heard of them. They were pretty big in the eighties but with all this revival stuff they got back together and have been permanently gigging for the last few years.'

A memory of Caroline gazing wistfully at the obituaries page of The Daily Telegraph popped into Poppy's mind.

'What band was it?'

'Cormac and the Sullivans. Why?'

Cloud goggled at the remains of a plastic bag caught on the branches of a hawthorn tree. Poppy clamped her legs to his sides and tightened her reins. 'It's a carrier bag, silly,' she told him. And then to Cameron, 'Was your dad the lead singer?'

'Yes. The late great Cormac O'Sullivan.'

'I have heard of him, actually. My stepmum had a crush on him when she was my age. She was so sad when he died.'

Cameron laughed hollowly. 'There will be hundreds, probably thousands, of middle-aged women in mourning. He was a big hit with the ladies. In fact he loved them almost as much as he loved music and horses.'

'You still haven't told me why you're here. Why you're so interested in Eddie Eaglestone and his stud. Why you suddenly forgot you were Irish just now.'

'When I was five we moved from Dublin to a farm in County Kildare. Dad's band had split up and he was working as a record producer. He told Mum he wanted space for a recording studio, but what he really wanted was space for his horses. He'd ridden as a teenager, but stopped when the band became successful. He'd promised himself that if the band ever split up he would buy a place in the country and start his own stud.

'Mum hated horses. She was terrified of them. But I loved them as much as Dad did. He bought me Bobby, a little Welsh Section A, to learn to ride on, and when I was older I had a Connemara called Maverick. Cloud reminds me of him a little.'

Poppy absentmindedly stroked Cloud's neck. She was wondering where Fearless Flight fitted in to all this.

'When I was seven, Dad and the band re-formed and went on a massive tour of the Middle East. He was away for weeks. They performed huge stadium concerts and private gigs for the oil magnates. He sent me photos of him riding Arab horses and camels in the desert.' Cameron reached in his pocket for the folded photocopy of the Arab yearling. 'He also sent me this.'

'Who is it?'

'It's a colt foal called The Persian. The photo was taken almost nine years ago. The Persian had impeccable breeding. In fact his bloodlines could be traced back to the Bedouin Arabians.'

'The same as Fearless Flight,' said Poppy, pleased to have remembered Eddie Eaglestone's description of his golden stallion.

'That's because Fearless Flight is The Persian,' said Cameron heavily.

Poppy laughed. 'Don't be silly. Of course he's not!'

'The Persian was auctioned as a yearling. Dad knew there'd be a bidding war but he was determined to buy him. He sold his Ferrari and Mum's Porsche to pay for him. She was absolutely furious.'

'But -' Poppy was desperate to point out that The Persian had a huge great diamond on his forehead and four white socks, and Fearless Flight did not.

'Dad flew The Persian home and we all fell in love with him. Even Mum. He was such a charismatic little fella. Then, when he was two, he was stolen. Dad was devastated. He blamed himself. But he also blamed our head groom.'

Poppy frowned. Why would a head groom steal a horse from his own yard? It didn't make sense. 'I don't understand.'

'The head groom had come over from England on a

temporary contract because our own head groom was out of action. D'you want to know where he came from?'

Poppy nodded.

'A brand new stud in Devon called Eaglestone Arabians. Quite a coincidence, wouldn't you say? Our head groom was Eaglestone's right hand man. Our head groom was Micky Murphy.'

27

The revelation sent Poppy's head spinning. But before she could quiz Cameron further, Hannah and Flynn dropped back to ride alongside them.

Hannah was fiddling with a hank of Flynn's bushy mane. 'How much further is it, Poppy? Flynn seems really tired this morning.'

Poppy gazed around her. She'd been so absorbed in Cameron's story that she hadn't taken any notice of their route, happy to let Scott and Sam lead the way. She stood up in her stirrups. In the distance the dark green blur of Hickman's Wood was a smudge on the horizon.

'It's this side of the wood. It should only take about a quarter of an hour, twenty minutes tops.'

'Not far now, angel,' Hannah crooned to Flynn. The little gelding's ears were pricked, but he seemed subdued. A lone magpie swooped across the path in front of them, chattering noisily. *One for sorrow*, thought Poppy.

'Good morning, Mr Magpie,' she said automatically.

'I hope the last clue isn't too far,' said Hannah.

'Eaglestone'll want us all back for the prizegiving at four

o'clock, won't he?' Poppy threw a meaningful glance at Cameron, who shrugged, kicked Floyd into a trot and joined Scott and Sam ahead.

'Not that we have a chance of winning now, thanks to Georgia,' said Hannah. 'They must be so far ahead I bet they're already on their way to the last clue. Do you know what the weird thing is?'

Poppy shook her head.

'It's a pretty straight line between the stud and Hickman's Wood, isn't it?'

'Due west,' she agreed.

'They must have taken a different route. It's so squelchy along here you'd see their footprints for sure. And I can tell you we're the first people to ride along here today.'

Poppy chewed her bottom lip. What if she was wrong and it wasn't Combe Falls at all? What if she was leading her friends on a wild goose chase? As if she was reading her mind, Hannah clapped her hand on her thigh. Flynn's ears flicked back.

'So what if we lose? It's been an adventure, right?' she grinned at Poppy.

Poppy smiled weakly back. 'It certainly has.'

THE SOUND of rushing water buzzed like static in their ears as they approached Combe Falls. The weir had been built in the late 18th century to create a mill pond, although the mill house it once served had long since crumbled to rubble. Upstream, the mill pond was deep and glassily still, diverging around a tiny island that was home to a family of otters, according to the visitor board in the nearby car park. Below, the water cascaded, fast and furiously, into a series of natural plunge pools where every autumn salmon began their heroic ascent upriver to spawn.

When the McKeevers had visited Combe Falls the banks of the river had been busy with anglers and walkers, but today the car park was empty and the riverside footpath deserted.

'Where d'you think the clue is?' said Hannah.

'There's a small bird-watching hide just above the weir. It must be there,' said Poppy. She jumped off Cloud and gave his reins to Hannah. 'You hold him. I'll go and look.'

The wooden hide was the size of a garden shed with a narrow window looking out over the river. Poppy pushed open the door and was hit by the smell of rotting leaves and damp timber. She shivered. Hidden from the sun by the canopy of trees, it was as cold as a cave. She scoured the hide for the familiar-looking wooden box, but it was empty, bar an old crisp packet and a polystyrene cup that had been abandoned on the slatted wooden bench.

Poppy's heart sank. She'd been wrong. The clue hadn't meant Combe Falls at all. There must be another river, another weir. She ducked back out of the hide and crossed the car park to the others, wondering how to break the bad news.

She decided there was no point sugar-coating it. 'I'm sorry,' she blurted. 'I got it wrong. It's not here.'

'You're joking,' said Scott.

'But you were so sure,' said Sam.

'I know and I'm sorry. But they must have meant somewhere else.'

Scarlett frowned. 'But there isn't anywhere else. Not on this part of the moor, anyway. Are you sure you looked properly?'

'Of course I did. Take a look yourself if you don't believe me,' said Poppy hotly.

Scarlett held up her hands. 'Alright, keep your hair on. I was only checking.'

'I hate the thought of giving up. Come on people, *think*. There must be another waterfall or weir,' said Scott. But the others were silent. If there was, no-one could think of it.

'So what do we do now?' said Cameron.

Poppy gave a helpless shrug. 'Admit defeat? We were never going to beat Georgia anyway. Not after this morning.'

'She's right,' said Sam. 'Let's take a vote. All those in favour of heading back to Eaglestone's place?'

Everyone raised a reluctant hand.

'Home it is,' said Hannah glumly. 'But first Flynn needs a drink.' She led the little gelding down to the water's edge. He lowered his head, sniffed the water and drank deeply. The others followed. Poppy gazed at their reflections in the mill pond. A splash of water made her look up and she gasped as a brown head, followed by a sleek brown body, popped out of the river onto the muddy bank of the little island opposite them.

She nudged Scarlett, held a finger to her lips and pointed to the bank. The otter was using its paws to groom itself like a cat. Cloud lifted his head, droplets of water splashing from his muzzle into the river like raindrops. At the sound the otter stopped, its head still and its nose twitching. With one fluid moment it ducked its head and disappeared back into the water with hardly a ripple.

'Wow,' said Poppy under her breath.

Scarlett was still staring at the island. Poppy followed her gaze. 'Is there another one?' she whispered.

Scarlett grinned at her. 'Not an otter, no. But there is a clue. Right there.'

28

The box was hanging from a small tree in the middle of the island.

'How on earth are we supposed to reach that?' said Hannah crossly.

The distance between the riverbank and the island was at least ten metres. If they crossed upstream of the weir there was little current but the water would be deep. How deep it was impossible to tell. Downstream of the weir the roar of the water was like white noise and the river pulsated through the rocky outcrops to the pools below like water gushing out of a firefighter's hose. Hidden rocks and the force of the current would make crossing below the weir treacherous.

The memory of another river nudged Poppy's subconscious and she was transported back to the wild and stormy night lightning had struck the stables at the end of her trekking holiday with Scarlett a couple of years before. Poppy and Beau, her horse for the week, had been racing to the nearest farm to raise the alarm when a bridge had collapsed beneath them, plunging them into a surging river, and they had almost drowned. Poppy shivered. The memory was so real she could taste the muddy river water. Instinctively, she took a step back from the riverbank.

'Flynn can swim,' said Scarlett suddenly. 'We took him and Blaze to the beach once, years ago. Blaze wouldn't go near the sea but Flynn loved it. I'll ride him across.'

Hannah crossed her arms. 'No way. If Flynn's going, then I'm riding him.'

'But I'm a better rider than you,' said Scarlett.

'And do I care?' Hannah's eyes flashed dangerously. 'He trusts me. I'll look after him. I'm going, OK? No arguments.'

'Hannah!' cried Poppy.

But Hannah had already whipped off Flynn's saddle and vaulted on. She gathered her reins and urged the little bay gelding into the river. He took one tentative step forward, snorted, and took another. Soon the water was knee height, then up to his elbow. He took another couple of paces and suddenly he was swimming.

Poppy shook her head in wonder. Flynn's nostrils and ears were above the water but otherwise he was completely submerged. Hannah's legs were wrapped tightly around his barrel-like body and her hands were entwined in his bushy mane.

'Are you alright?' Poppy called anxiously.

'Are you kidding? This is brilliant! Flynn is brilliant!' She threw her head back and laughed.

Under the water Flynn's legs must have been working like pistons because soon he was scrambling onto the bank on the other side of the river. He shook himself, sending a shower of water over Hannah. She looked down at her sodden teeshirt and jodhpurs and laughed again. Poppy felt a surge of affection for her friend. She looked nothing like the city slick girl who'd turned up at Riverdale a week ago sporting a choppy blonde bob, dusky pink cardigan and denim miniskirt.

'Great job you two!' Poppy shouted across the water.

'Just one minor problem. You were in such a hurry you forgot to take the cards,' called Scott.

'Oops,' said Hannah with a sheepish grin. 'Don't worry, we'll bring the whole box back.'

She led Flynn over to the small tree the box was dangling from. Poppy could hear her humming to herself as she opened the box and peered inside. The humming stopped. Frowning, Hannah held the box upside down and gave it a shake. Nothing fell out.

'What's wrong?' called Scarlett.

Hannah held the box open with outstretched arms. 'There's nothing in there. No clue, no stamp, nothing. It's empty.'

Scarlett shook her head in disbelief. 'I didn't think even Georgia Canning would stoop that low.'

'We don't know if it was definitely her,' Poppy reasoned.

'Who else would it be - the endurance women? I don't think so.'

'Scarlett's right. You know how competitive she is,' said Sam.

'But still -' said Poppy, wondering why she was so keen to defend Georgia.

'Some people have to win at all costs. They don't worry who they step on in the process.' Scott tightened Troy's girth and pulled down his stirrups. 'I'm going to head back. I've got an early start in the morning.'

Cameron nodded. 'I'll come with you. Sam, are you coming?'

Sam hesitated. 'Maybe I should stay with the girls? Make sure they get back safely.'

Scarlett bristled. 'We managed just fine on our own before you decided to tag along,' she said hotly.

Sam raised his eyebrows at Poppy.

'We'll be fine, honestly. You go.'

'If you're sure.' Sam jumped lightly into the saddle. 'See you back at the stud for the prize giving?'

Poppy smiled. 'I'll be there.'

Over on the island Hannah was wrestling with the rope tying the box to the tree. 'I want to bring it back as evidence that Georgia cheated,' she puffed. 'But the knot's so tight.' She coaxed Flynn under the box and climbed onto his back. Holding his mane with one hand and the box in the other, she used her teeth to loosen the knot. 'There!' she said with satisfaction as the rope finally slid free.

'Are you coming or what?' shouted Scarlett.

'On my way,' Hannah called. She clasped the box under her right arm and held her reins in her left hand. Clicking her tongue, she guided Flynn back down the river bank. It was only as the bay gelding stepped into the water that Poppy realised how much closer they were to the wall of the weir.

Beside her, Cloud had stopped nibbling the sparse grass on the riverbank and was watching Flynn as he swam towards them. The current was faster by the weir and Flynn didn't seem to be making much headway.

Poppy gripped Cloud's reins. 'You alright?' she called across to Hannah.

'He's tired, that's all. I'm getting off,' Hannah called back.

Poppy took a couple of steps forward, hardly noticing the chilly river water swirling around her jodhpur boots. 'Are you sure that's a good idea?'

But Hannah had already jumped off and was swimming beside Flynn. She was a strong swimmer. Poppy could remember her on the podium with a clutch of medals around her neck at their primary school's annual swimming gala. Even though she was still gripping the box in one hand it wasn't long before she had overtaken the gelding. She turned back and trod water until he caught her up.

As he reached her his head disappeared under the water just for a second. He surfaced with a splash, his eyes rolling and his ears glistening with water.

'Come on, little man,' crooned Hannah. 'We're nearly there.' She turned in the water and began swimming towards them. But Poppy could see just how tired the little Dartmoor was. His head dipped under the water again and this time when he surfaced his eyes were white with terror.

Scarlett's hand flew to her mouth. They watched, horrified, as a surge in the current caught the Dartmoor pony off guard and carried him inexorably towards the weir.

29

'Hannah!' screamed Poppy.

Hannah lunged for the cheekpiece on Flynn's bridle. When her fingers closed around it Poppy thought everything might be OK, that she'd be able to pull Flynn back from the brink. But the old leather was brittle and snapped in two. With a high-pitched whinny, Flynn was swept over the wall of the weir into the rocky pools below.

Poppy flung Cloud's reins at Scarlett and waded into the water above the weir. She pulled Hannah out and together they raced downstream.

'He's going to drown,' Hannah sobbed.

Poppy thought it was more likely that he'd break a leg on the rocks, but she kept the thought to herself. They reached the bottom of the weir where the water roiled and bubbled like the Atlantic in a Force 10 gale. Spray hit her eyes, clouding her vision, so at first she couldn't see the gelding at all.

'Where is he?' she yelled to Hannah.

'There, by the rocks.'

Poppy rubbed her eyes and followed Hannah's gaze.

Flynn was on his side being battered by the torrent of water slicing relentlessly over the top of the weir. At the sound of their voices he struggled to his feet. *Please let him be OK*, Poppy thought. She'd learnt to ride on Flynn. He'd stood patiently as she'd learnt to groom him and tack him up. He hadn't protested when she'd bumped around on his back, trying to master a rising trot. The more proficient she'd become, the more he'd tested her. He was the perfect school-master and she wouldn't be the rider she was today if it wasn't for him. She owed him so much. Tears streamed down her cheeks, mingling with spray from the river, as she struggled through the swirling water towards him.

It was treacherous. Rocks as sharp as razors lay in wait just under the surface, ready to graze their legs if they slipped. Once Hannah lost her footing and would have hurtled into the river headfirst had Poppy not shot out an arm to steady her.

On the riverbank Cloud whinnied, the noise amplified by the canopy of trees. Flynn whinnied back, a faint echo of Cloud's call. The sound tugged on Poppy's heartstrings.

Finally they reached him. Hannah threw her arms around him. 'You're OK!' she cried.

But Poppy had seen the pink water surging around their legs. He must be cut to smithereens. What if the rocks had damaged a tendon?

'We need to get him out of the water,' she said urgently.

His bit hung uselessly from the one remaining cheek-piece. Poppy carefully pulled the headpiece over his ears. The reins were still looped around his neck and she gave them a gentle tug.

'Come on, Flynn. Let's get you out of the river,' she said.

Flynn took a shaky step forward, then stopped. His ears flicked back and forth as the water flowed past.

Poppy clicked her tongue. 'There's a good lad, keep going.'

He took another unsteady step, and another. Then he lost his footing and stumbled forward, his muzzle dipping under the water. Poppy tugged his reins again but he refused to budge. Hannah shot Poppy a desperate look.

'How can we help him?'

Poppy thought hard. 'You pull, I'll push.' She handed Hannah the reins and what was left of his bridle and waded through the water to his hindquarters. 'On the count of three, OK?'

Hannah nodded.

'One…two…THREE!'

Poppy braced her legs against a rock, leant against Flynn's broad rump and pushed with all her might while Hannah coaxed him forward. When he didn't move a muscle Poppy felt panic grip her insides. But then he took one wobbly step, and another, and she felt a glimmer of hope that they'd make it.

'That's it! Keep him going!' Scarlett shouted.

Hannah kept coaxing and Poppy kept pushing. Step by tentative step the little bay gelding negotiated the rocks and crashing water. Finally he reached the riverbank.

'Almost there,' Scarlett called. 'Come on, Flynn. You can do it!'

It was a tough clamber up from this side of the weir and Poppy wasn't sure he'd make it. But it was as if he'd realised he was almost home and dry. He bowed his head and scrabbled up, his legs flailing as they fought to gain a foothold on the muddy bank. He gave an almighty shake, sending water droplets flying.

'We n-need to ch-check his legs,' said Poppy through chattering teeth.

'You hold these two,' said Scarlett, handing her Cloud's and Red's reins. She bent down and examined Flynn's legs one by one.

'Well?' said Hannah anxiously.

Scarlett straightened her back and rested a hand on Flynn's withers. 'There's a nasty tear on his near hind leg. It might need a stitch or two but it doesn't look too deep.' She glanced at the river. 'At least it should be clean.'

'So what do we do now?' said Poppy.

Flynn stood with his legs slightly splayed and his head bowed. Exhaustion oozed out of every pore. There was no way he would make it back to Eaglestone Arabians and for once Poppy was all out of ideas.

'I need to call Dad. Ask him to bring the trailer over,' said Scarlett. She checked her mobile and shook her head. 'No signal. What about you two?'

'Mine's completely dead,' said Poppy.

'Use mine,' said Hannah, pulling her phone out and holding her thumb over the fingerprint sensor. 'Wait, it's not turning on.' She gave the phone a little shake and tried again. 'It's still not working.'

'Give it to me,' said Scarlett. She peered at the phone. 'There's water under the screen. You must have got it wet.'

'So how are you going to call your Dad?' Hannah cried.

'I'll go after the boys,' said Poppy suddenly.

'But they must have been gone almost half an hour,' said Scarlett.

Poppy tweaked Cloud's ear. 'That's alright. We'll catch them up. You two stay here with Flynn.'

Hearing his name, Flynn's head shot up, as if he had woken from a trance. He whickered softly and nudged Hannah's sodden jodhpurs. She laughed and the other two grinned back.

'Here you are,' she said, offering him a couple of soggy pony nuts which he guzzled as if he hadn't eaten for days.

'And that's why Dartmoor ponies are known for their hardiness,' said Scarlett sagely.

Poppy stood on one foot and emptied the contents of one jodhpur boot back into the river, then repeated the process with the other boot. She wrung out her teeshirt as best she could, tightened Cloud's girth, pulled down the stirrups and hauled herself into the saddle.

'I'll be as quick as I can,' she promised.

Cloud's ears were pricked as they walked through the car park and past the bird hide. Once they were back on the path Poppy squeezed him into a canter, marvelling at how willing he was after such a long and tiring two days. Before long they had reached the open moor and she eased him back into a walk so she could check her bearings. The last thing she needed was to get lost now. She stood up in her stirrups and scanned the moor. Her heart lifted when her eyes locked onto three tiny shapes on the horizon. It had to be them. She kicked Cloud back into a canter and crouched low over his neck as his stride lengthened. Soon they were galloping across the moor, boulders and the occasional sheep blurring as they raced past. The wind ruffled Cloud's silver mane and his tail streamed behind him like a pennant. The anxiety of the last half an hour was replaced with a buzz of pure exhilaration.

Georgia would probably win the treasure hunt and take home the golden horse. But Poppy didn't care. Flynn was alright. That was all that really mattered.

30

Star was the first to hear them. The black mare turned her head and whinnied as Cloud galloped towards them. Poppy heard Sam call out to the others and they swivelled around in their saddles as she approached.

Scott frowned. 'I thought you were staying with the girls?'

Poppy pulled Cloud up alongside them and tried to catch her breath.

'It's Flynn,' she panted. 'He fell when he was crossing the river. He's OK, but he'll never make it back to the stud. We need to phone Scarlett's dad to get him to bring the trailer over, but none of our phones were working.'

Sam was already reaching for his mobile. 'I can do better than that. I'll ask Gran. They'll all fit in the lorry.' He held the phone to his ear. 'Gran? It's me. Change of plan.'

After explaining their predicament Sam ended the call. 'It's all sorted. She's going to pick Flynn and Red up from the car park at Combe Falls and then head over to Eaglestone's place to pick us up. She'll drop you guys home.'

Poppy checked her watch. It was almost one. They should

have enough time to settle the ponies at home and be back at the stud by four o'clock.

'Are you going to the prize-giving?' she asked.

'Nah, waste of time,' said Scott.

Sam shook his head. 'I don't think I can be bothered now, either.'

'What about you, Cameron?'

Cameron smiled thinly. 'I wouldn't miss it for the world. Eaglestone and I have some unfinished business to sort out.'

WITH SAM and Scott riding a little way ahead Poppy seized the opportunity to grill Cameron.

'You're not planning to confront Eaglestone at the prize-giving are you?'

Cameron pulled a face. 'Why not? It's the perfect opportunity. Plenty of people to witness his confession. With any luck that reporter and photographer will be there again, too.'

'You can't!' Poppy cried, aghast. 'He'll have you for slander. You've got no evidence!'

Cameron's eyes narrowed. 'Don't you believe me?'

'Of course I do!' Poppy blurted. 'No-one would make up a story like that.'

'The man's a thief, Poppy. He stole The Persian from my dad and I want him back.'

Poppy chewed her lip. She needed to broach the huge discrepancy in Cameron's story. The elephant in the room. She took a deep breath. 'That picture of The Persian you carry around with you -' she began hesitantly.

'What about it?'

'He had a blaze and four white socks. Fearless Flight hasn't. Horses don't just lose their markings.'

Cameron gave an impatient tsk. 'I'm not stupid. Eaglestone's disguised him, obviously.'

'Disguised him?'

'Haven't you ever heard of hair dye?'

'But how will you prove it?'

'Not long after The Persian arrived on the farm he became cast in his stable. He was fine, apart from a cut below his near fetlock. It was small, but deep. He had it stitched and it healed well, but it left him with a tiny scar shaped like a crescent moon. I went into Fearless Flight's stable last night to check. The scar is there, Poppy, just as I remembered. He's The Persian alright.'

'Can you prove he had that injury when he was a yearling?'

'Hey, wait a minute, who's on trial here, me or Eaglestone?'

'I'm trying to help, Cameron. Think. Is there anyone else who could corroborate your story?'

'Sure, the vet would have a record of his visit, wouldn't he?'

Poppy nodded. 'Once we're home we'll contact the surgery, ask them to send it over. Then we can go to the police.'

'They weren't much use when The Persian was stolen.'

'You don't know that. They may have had their suspicions about Micky Murphy at the time but didn't have enough evidence to arrest him.' As Poppy spoke, a plan began to form in her mind. It was audacious and fraught with danger, but if they pulled it off it could give them all the evidence they could possibly need.

They had almost reached the turning to the stud.

Cameron halted Floyd. 'So how do we find the evidence?'

Poppy smiled. 'Funny you should ask. I've had an idea.'

ONCE AGAIN THE stud was a hive of activity as Eddie Eagle-stone's staff prepared for the prize-giving ceremony. As Poppy followed the boys up the drive she noticed the only two other teams left in the competition, Georgia and her friends and the three endurance riders, waiting in the field they'd camped in the previous night. Poppy stared at her feet, hoping Georgia hadn't seen her, but no such luck.

'Why, if it isn't Poppy McKeever,' the older girl drawled. She handed Barley's reins to Fiona and stalked over, her eyes widening in surprise as she took in Poppy's dishevelled state.

'You look like you've been dragged through a hedge - or should I say river - backwards. Where on earth have you been?'

'I'm surprised you need to ask,' said Poppy levelly.

Georgia narrowed her eyes. 'What d'you mean?'

Poppy felt anger stir in the pit of her stomach. 'You hid our tack and took the clue at Combe Falls. What d'you think I mean?'

A flicker of surprise clouded Georgia's perfect features. She held up her hands in surrender. 'OK, so we hid your tack, but that was to pay you back for sending us in the wrong direction to Witch Cottage. I'd say you deserved it. And we only wanted to give ourselves a head start. We knew you'd find it pretty quickly. But we haven't even been to Combe Falls, so how can we have taken a clue from there?'

'What d'you mean, you haven't been to Combe Falls?' said Poppy sharply.

'The clue sent us to the clapper bridge at Fourways.'

'Which clue?'

'The one at Witch Cottage,' said Georgia, speaking slowly as if she was talking to an imbecile.

'Well, it sent us to Combe Falls.'

'Are you sure?'

'Of course I'm sure! And Flynn fell crossing the river. He could have broken a leg! So the next time you play dirty, perhaps you should consider the consequences.'

'I just told you. We didn't. Can you remember the clue?'

Salmons leap, The wild ones swim. Above I am still, Below full of vim,' Poppy recited.

'That's not the clue we had,' said Georgia. 'And the clue at Fourways sent us to the top of Worthy Tor.' She paused for dramatic effect. 'Which is where we found the golden horse.'

Poppy's shoulders sagged. 'You won, then.'

'The endurance riders were fast but they don't know the moor like I do. And with you lot out of the way it was in the bag.' Georgia's eyes gleamed with triumph.

Poppy knew she'd decided on the way over that she didn't care if Georgia won or not, she was just glad Flynn was OK. But she'd clean forgotten how insufferable the older girl could be. Right now she'd give anything to wipe the smug look off her face. But to show her frustration would be to show weakness.

She straightened her back and cleared her throat. 'Congratulations,' she said.

'You're muttering. I didn't hear you,' said Georgia, cupping her ear.

'I said congratulations,' said Poppy loudly, before turning on her heels and pulling Cloud towards the stables.

She'd almost caught up with the boys when Georgia called, 'Poppy, wait a minute!'

'What does she want now,' she grumbled to Cloud.

Georgia ran over. She locked eyes with Poppy. 'Our clue led us to Fourways, I promise. We never went near Combe Falls. Whoever led you on a wild goose chase, it wasn't us.'

31

P oppy didn't have time to wonder what Georgia's declaration meant, because a familiar-looking steel-grey horse lorry was rumbling into the yard. Bella Thompson, the indomitable owner of Redhall Manor Equestrian Centre and Sam's gran, jumped down from the cab followed closely by Scarlett and Hannah.

'Flynn OK?' Poppy asked them.

Hannah smiled. 'He went straight up the ramp and is now demolishing a hay net almost as big as he is.'

'Bella's checked his legs and doesn't think that cut needs a stitch. I've just got to keep it clean and check it doesn't become infected,' said Scarlett.

'I'm going to help, aren't I, Scar? At least until I go home,' said Hannah.

Scarlett smiled gratefully at Hannah and Poppy's eyebrows shot up. Had her two friends finally decided to bury the hatchet - and not in each other?

'Righto, you lot. I have a lesson at five. Let's get this show on the road,' said Bella.

Hannah and Scarlett ran across to the field shelter to

fetch their tents and the rest of their equipment while Poppy and the boys untacked the four horses and led them up the ramp one by one.

Soon all six were inside. Scott and Sam heaved up the ramp and joined Bella in the cab. Poppy, Scarlett, Hannah and Cameron strapped themselves into the two bench seats in the living accommodation. Poppy told them about Georgia, Fiona and Lucy finding the golden horse and Georgia's claim that they hadn't messed with the clues.

Scarlett was sceptical. 'But she would say that, wouldn't she?'

'And if they didn't, who did?' said Hannah.

Cameron shrugged. 'I'd have thought that was pretty obvious.'

'The endurance riders?' Scarlett scoffed. 'I'm telling you, it was Georgia Canning. The girl who can't bear to lose.'

Cameron met Poppy's eye. He thought it was Eaglestone, she realised suddenly. Eaglestone or his sidekick Micky Murphy. And Murphy had been at Witch Cottage. Had he switched the clue, sending them to the swollen river at Combe Falls, and then switched it back again for the final two teams? It was conceivable. But if so, why? The unwelcome suspicion that he might know who Cameron was and why he was here wormed its way into Poppy's head. If he did, their plan wouldn't just be foolhardy, it would be downright dangerous.

'Let's not bother going to the prize-giving,' said Hannah. 'I'm going home tomorrow. I'd rather spend the rest of the afternoon with Flynn.'

'Hear hear,' said Scarlett. 'Who wants to watch Georgia lording over everyone as usual anyway? I certainly don't.'

Poppy felt her patience snap and she glared at Scarlett. 'For goodness sake, will you just drop it? Georgia gave me her word she didn't switch the clues and I believe her. So swallow your pride and come.'

Scarlett scowled back. 'You're supposed to be my best friend. You always take her side!'

'Don't be ridiculous. Of course I don't,' said Poppy hotly.

'Come now, children, stop your bickering,' said Cameron. 'We all need to go to the prize-giving, OK? We need to find out who sent us on a fool's errand.'

As Redhall was nearer than Waterby, Bella dropped Floyd, Troy and Star off first. While Scott settled the horses and Cameron thanked Bella for lending her Floyd, Sam came to say goodbye.

'It's a shame we didn't win, but it was still good fun,' he said.

'It was,' agreed Poppy, although her stomach was churning at the thought of the task ahead.

'See you again?' he asked Hannah.

'You bet! Poppy won't be able to keep me away. I'll ask Mum if I can come down for a week in the summer holidays.'

'Cool.' He addressed Poppy and Scarlett. 'See you both Thursday?'

It was the day they shared a jumping lesson. Poppy nodded. Sam flashed her a smile and ducked out of the door.

'Let's hope you're talking to each other by then,' said Hannah archly.

Poppy felt a giggle rise up her throat and burst out before she could swallow it down. Hannah sniggered. Scarlett let out a most unladylike snort. Soon all three were howling with laughter. Poppy gasped for breath, her whole body convulsing.

'Enough!' she cried, wiping the tears from her cheeks. But her plea set them off again and they clutched their sides until their fit of the giggles had worn itself out.

Hannah regarded her two friends fondly. 'You two are so

funny. Just when me and Scar work it out you fall out with each other. Talk about two's company, three's a crowd.'

Poppy and Scarlett gave each other sheepish looks.

'Sorry,' they said in unison.

'Best friends forever?' said Poppy.

Scarlett dipped her head. 'Always,' she said. 'But something else, too.' She held out her fist. 'The Three Amigos.'

Poppy looked quizzically at Hannah.

'I taught her while we were waiting for Bella. You don't mind, do you?'

Poppy grinned. 'Of course not. I've spent the last week wishing you'd be friends.'

She and Hannah held out their fists. They tapped. Tapped again and bumped. Followed through with a high five and jazz fingers. They pealed with laughter.

'To The Three Amigos,' Hannah spluttered.

Poppy and Scarlett raised their hands, as if drinking a toast. 'The Three Amigos!' they cried.

CAMERON SAT in the cab with Bella on the way to Waterby and Poppy took the opportunity to tell Scarlett and Hannah about The Persian and how Micky Murphy had stolen him all those years ago. They listened, open-mouthed, as Poppy described how Cameron had come over from Ireland with the express purpose of exposing the theft and claiming back The Persian.

'He wants to confront Eaglestone in front of everyone this afternoon. I've told him it's all circumstantial and that he needs hard proof. And so I've had an idea. But we'll need your help.'

'Name it,' said Hannah, goggle-eyed.

'Anything,' said Scarlett.

The two girls were silent as Poppy outlined her plan.

'It's inspired,' said Hannah.

'It's downright dangerous,' said Scarlett.

'I know,' said Poppy heavily. 'But don't you see? It's the only way.'

32

Exhaustion hit Poppy like a wave as she led Cloud into his stable. She brushed it aside - there was no time to be tired. She mixed him a feed and set to work grooming him from his ears to his tail, brushing off the dried sweat until his dapple grey coat shone. Once she'd finished she turned him out in the paddock. Chester and Jenny ambled over and touched noses with the Connemara. Jenny gave a soft hee-haw and Cloud whickered and nuzzled her neck. Poppy wondered if he was telling them about his adventures on the hunt for the golden horse. There was a lot to tell, and the story wasn't over yet. When all three wandered off to graze Poppy trudged back to the house.

Charlie appeared from the back door, Freddie at his feet. Poppy bent down to fuss the dog, who immediately lay down and offered her his tummy to rub.

'Where's Hannah?' Charlie demanded.

'Welcome home, Poppy. How did the treasure hunt go?' said Poppy sarcastically.

Charlie tutted. 'Welcome home, sis. How did the treasure hunt go? Did you win? And where's Hannah?'

'It was, er, interesting, and no, we didn't win. Georgia Canning and her friends did. And Hannah's over at Ashworthy, helping Scarlett with Flynn.'

'Mum says you need to leave by half three at the latest if you're going to be on time for the presentation.'

'Aren't you coming?'

'No room in the car, not if Cameron's going, too. Bill's going to teach me to drive Little Fergie.'

Poppy raised her eyebrows at the thought of Charlie behind the wheel of Bill's grey Ferguson tractor. She thought she and Cameron were venturing into dangerous territory. But facing Eaglestone would be a walk in the park compared to teaching her adrenalin junkie brother to drive. Bill needed his head testing.

As THEY DROVE along the lanes towards Eaglestone Arabians Poppy went through the plan in her head. She'd told Cameron they needed concrete proof that Eddie Eaglestone had stolen The Persian. But she had no idea what form this hard evidence might take. An old diary detailing the theft? Highly unlikely. A handy signed confession? As if. She just hoped that she'd know what she was looking for when she found it. In other words, she was completely winging it. It wouldn't be the first time, she thought wryly.

Caroline pulled in through the stud's double gates and the car bumped slowly down the drive. Poppy felt her heartbeat quicken and she glanced at Cameron. He was staring straight ahead, the angular set of his jawline as rigid as steel. She wondered if he was as nervous as she was.

Caroline, who had arranged to meet a friend for coffee at a nearby garden centre, turned in her seat. 'I'll drop you here, if that's OK?'

'Of course. Thanks Mum. We'll see you at five,' said Poppy.

The four teenagers waved blithely as Caroline executed a perfect three point turn and headed back down the drive.

'This subterfuge lark is quite stressful, isn't it?' said Hannah out of the corner of her mouth.

'You're not kidding.' Scarlett, checking no-one was in earshot, grabbed Poppy's arm and stage whispered, 'We'll text you when he looks like he's beginning to wind up, OK?'

Poppy nodded and patted her back pocket. 'It's on silent but I'll feel it vibrate,' she whispered back. And then the blood drained from her face and she groaned.

'What is it?' said Hannah.

'What an idiot. I forgot to charge it.'

'I can't help. Mine's completely dead and we need Scarlett's to text you,' said Hannah. 'What about your phone, Cameron?'

He fished it out of his pocket. 'It's on twenty per cent,' he said.

Poppy swallowed. 'It'll have to do.'

Once again a semi-circle of foldable chairs had been set up in the middle of the lawn. In front of them was a table with a white linen tablecloth over. On it stood the small prancing golden horse they'd spent the last two days hunting.

Poppy's eyes were drawn to the flesh and bone golden horse they were really here to see. But Fearless Flight's stable was bolted closed. She felt a frisson of fear. What if Eddie Eaglestone had second-guessed them and knew what they were planning? It was a chance they'd have to take.

'We'll see you later,' said Hannah, dragging Scarlett towards the chairs. Georgia, Fiona and Lucy had already bagged the front row and behind them Sniffer Smith, holding both a notebook and a camera, sat next to the three endurance riders. Poppy quickly scanned the remaining rows. The three boys were there, minus their cobs, as was the team from the riding school near Okehampton. There were a handful more faces she didn't recognise.

Poppy and Cameron hung back as Eddie Eaglestone strode onto the lawn, followed closely by his head groom. Micky Murphy's face was inscrutable as he handed his boss the microphone.

'Welcome back to Eaglestone Arabians, and I hope you enjoyed my challenge,' Eaglestone began.

Poppy felt a hand on her arm.

'Come on,' whispered Cameron. 'We haven't got long.'

33

They slipped away towards the house as stealthily as cat burglars.

'I bet the back door is open,' said Cameron once they were safely out of earshot.

Poppy's heart was thudding in her chest.

'How long d'you think we've got?'

'At least fifteen minutes. You know how much Eaglestone likes the sound of his own voice.'

They paused outside the sturdy back door.

'Ready?' said Cameron.

'Ready,' said Poppy. She stepped forward and tried the door knob but her palm was so sweaty it didn't move an inch. She wiped her hand on her jodhpurs and tried again. This time there was a click and the door creaked open.

They found themselves in a boot room. A door to their right led to a small cloakroom and to their left was the kitchen.

'We need to find his study,' said Cameron. 'Follow me.'

They passed a large lounge and a dining room with a magnificent chandelier suspended over a polished mahogany table large enough to seat at least twenty. Ahead was a sweeping staircase and to the left of that was a wood panelled wall.

'Perhaps it's upstairs,' said Cameron, his foot on the bottom tread.

'No, wait.' Poppy had noticed a rectangle-shaped groove in the panelling. 'There's a hidden door, look.'

Cameron was by her side in a flash. He ran his hands over the oak panelling, feeling for pressure points. He grinned at Poppy as the door sprung open. 'Clever girl.'

Poppy pushed past him into Eddie Eaglestone's study. The walls were covered with photos and portraits of Arab horses. In pride of place above the fireplace was a vast oil painting of a familiar-looking light chestnut stallion.

'Fearless Flight,' Poppy whispered.

'The Persian,' Cameron corrected her. He began rifling through a pile of papers on an oak coffee table. 'What are we looking for?'

Poppy headed for the desk. 'Anything that links Eaglestone to your dad or The Persian. Horse passports, fake documents, that kind of thing.'

She gazed at the expensive-looking laptop on Eaglestone's desk and the untidy pile of paperwork beside it. She began half-heartedly flicking through the papers, but they were just feed bills and invoices.

'Nothing here,' she said.

'Try the drawers,' said Cameron urgently.

Poppy hesitated. It seemed so intrusive. But an image of The Persian, still a leggy two-year-old colt, flitted across her mind. He had been so young when Eddie Eaglestone had stolen him. Still a baby, really. He must have been terrified. Poppy hardened her resolve and pulled open the top drawer.

The familiar masthead of The Daily Telegraph was poking out from beneath a Chinese takeaway menu and a copy of the Racing Post. Her heart in her mouth, Poppy pulled it out and checked the date. The twenty-fourth of May. She counted back on her fingers, shaking her head in disbelief. It was the day she had found Caroline reading the obituary of Cormac O'Sullivan.

She found the obituary page and there he was. Caroline's teenage crush, Cameron's dad and the owner of The Persian, staring at her appraisingly with those cool, green eyes.

'Cameron, you need to see this.'

He was by her side in a flash, the colour leaching from his face as he saw his dad staring back at him from the pages of the newspaper. His eyes narrowed as he skim-read the article and then he stabbed the newsprint with his index finger.

'There's our proof.'

'What do you mean?' said Poppy.

'It's obvious. Eaglestone has been wanting recognition for his stud for years, but he's had to carry on behind closed doors all the time Dad was alive. He knew that if Dad ever saw a photo of The Persian he would recognise him immediately. He worshipped that horse.'

'You're saying he was waiting for your dad to die,' said Poppy slowly.

'That's exactly what I'm saying. With Dad safely out of the way he could throw open the doors of Eaglestone Arabians and invite the world in without the fear of being exposed as a common thief.'

'But he hadn't reckoned on you making the connection.'

'No,' said Cameron grimly. 'Fortunately he has no idea who I am.' He reached in his back pocket for his phone and took a couple of photos of the newspaper on Eddie's desk. Poppy folded it and stuffed it back in the drawer. As she did a sheet of paper caught her eye. It was a list of the people taking part in the treasure hunt. Her name was there, sandwiched between Scarlett's and Hannah's. Sam and Scott's names were also there. But her eye was drawn to a name at the bottom that had been underlined in red three times. The lines had been so deeply scored they reminded Poppy of scars. It was as though someone had attacked the paper with a knife, not a pen. The fury behind them was unmistakable.

Cameron was already striding towards the door.

'Cam,' Poppy called. 'What's your last name?'

'Walsh,' he said.

Poppy swallowed. 'Not O'Sullivan?'

'My parents never married. I took Mum's name. Why?'

Poppy held up the list of names with a trembling hand. 'I'm afraid Eddie does know exactly who you are.'

Cameron's phone buzzed in his pocket.

'It's Scarlett,' he said. 'She reckons we have another five minutes.'

Poppy shoved the list back in the drawer and slammed it shut. Cameron was already disappearing through the door and she sprinted after him. They ran through the house and out of the back door. Cameron glanced left and right and, satisfied the coast was clear, nodded towards the back of the stable block. Poppy scooted after him.

They leant against the brick wall catching their breath. In the distance they could hear a ripple of applause coming from the yard.

Cameron started tapping at his mobile.

'What are you doing?' said Poppy sharply.

'Calling the police, what d'you think?'

Poppy grabbed his arm. 'We still haven't got any proof!'

Cameron's eyes blazed dangerously. 'Of course we have. Why else would Eaglestone have a copy of Dad's obituary in his study?'

'It's all circumstantial. How do you know he doesn't read

The Telegraph every day? We need hard evidence before we call the police, Cam. Surely you can see that?'

The fight went out of him as suddenly as if someone had flicked a switch and he ran a hand across his face. 'So what do we do?'

Poppy patted him gingerly on the shoulder. 'We think outside the box.'

'And how's that going to help?'

But Poppy was on a roll. 'We need to forget about looking for eight-year-old clues. We need to look at the evidence we have now.'

'Like what?'

Poppy held Cameron's eye. 'The Persian, of course.'

Poppy beckoned Cameron to follow her and they edged their way along the block of stables until they reached the tack room at the end. She peered around the corner. In the centre of the yard Eddie Eaglestone was presenting the golden horse to Georgia Canning and her team-mates while Sniffer Smith fiddled with his lens and started snapping away.

'We'll check his stable first,' said Poppy.

'What if Eaglestone sees us?' said Cameron.

'Don't worry, I've got an idea. Give me your phone.' Poppy glanced over to the small crowd watching the presentation. Scarlett was chatting to Hannah at the back. She tapped out a message.

Scar, we need to check something else out. Can you and Hannah distract Eaglestone for ten mins?

She watched as Scarlett checked her phone, whispered something to Hannah and typed a message back. The phone vibrated in her hand.

Of course. You OK?

We're fine, don't worry. But I think Eaglestone knows Cameron's onto him.

Poppy could see Scarlett shoot a worried look at Hannah and start typing furiously.

Be careful Poppy!!!

I will, I promise x

A few feet away from Scarlett, Sniffer Smith squinted at the photos on the back of his camera and gave Eddie and Georgia the thumbs up. Poppy held her breath as Scarlett grabbed Hannah's hand and marched over to the stud owner.

'Scarlett and Hannah are going to distract Eaglestone. And they can both talk for England. We should be good for at least ten minutes,' she whispered to Cameron.

'So what are we waiting for?'

Heads down, they set off for The Persian's stable. Adrenalin coursed through Poppy's veins as she glanced back at the little knot of people in the middle of the yard. Eddie Eaglestone was holding court, Scarlett and Hannah hanging onto his every word. She eased the top bolt across and pulled the door open.

But the chestnut stallion's huge loose box was empty.

Cameron kicked the door in frustration. 'He's gone and it's all my fault. I've made him too hot to handle.'

Poppy held a finger to her lips. They both listened as a muffled whinny rumbled through the air like a grumble of thunder from a distant storm. It was coming from the stud's huge barn.

They looked at each other.

'The Persian!' they whispered in unison.

Seconds later they were standing in front of the barn's double doors. Poppy took a deep breath and pushed them open. It was dark inside and her eyes took a moment to adjust. She could just make out a towering stack of hay to her left and bales of shavings stacked neatly to her right. Her nerves felt jangled and her senses on hyper-alert.

When Cameron gave a low whistle Poppy almost jumped out of her skin.

'What did you do that for?' she cried.

But Cameron gave a dismissive wave of his hand and whistled again. This time there was an answering whicker from the far side of the barn. The hairs on the back of Poppy's neck stood up. She felt in her pocket for the handkerchief Caroline had given her before they'd set off on the treasure hunt. It seemed like weeks ago. Was it really only yesterday?

Cameron tiptoed towards a shaft of sunlight at the far end of the barn. His movements were so exaggerated he reminded Poppy of a character in a cartoon and she had the sudden urge to giggle. She hurriedly turned the giggle into a cough, but not before Cameron swung around and hissed, 'Shush!'

'Sorry,' Poppy mouthed.

There in front of them, the light from the tiny window in the eaves of the barn turning his coat golden, was The Persian. He whickered again and nuzzled Cameron's pockets. The Arab stallion really was magnificent, from the tips of his curved ears to his powerful quarters.

Poppy leaned on the wooden partition that had transformed the end of the barn into a huge loose box. 'I'd forgotten how beautiful he is,' she breathed.

She spied a head collar on a grey plastic grooming box in the corner.

'D'you reckon you can get that on him? There's something I need to do.'

'Sure.' Cameron grabbed the head collar and approached the stallion quietly, talking to him in a low voice all the time.

'Hey Big Man, that's what Dad used to call you, isn't it? Do you remember him?' he held out a hand and the stallion extended his neck and sniffed his palm. Cameron smiled. ''Atta boy. I reckon you do. I'm just going to put this head collar on you, OK? Nothing to be frightened of.' He slipped on the noseband and fastened the headpiece in one fluid movement.

Poppy spat several times on her handkerchief. 'Not very ladylike I know, but needs must. Note to self: Must put my name down for that Swiss finishing school Dad's always on about.'

'Who on earth are you talking to?'

'Sorry, just a bit nervous, you know? What if we're wrong?'

'We're not wrong,' said Cameron firmly.

Poppy showed the handkerchief to The Persian. He snorted a couple of times but didn't pull back. Encouraged, she stepped closer, smoothed his long forelock out of the way and began rubbing the cotton against his forehead in a gentle, circular motion.

'Anything?' said Cameron.

Poppy examined the hankie. It was still resolutely white. She spat and rubbed, spat and rubbed, until her arm was aching and her mouth was dry.

'It's not working!'

'Hold him. I've got an idea.' Cameron handed Poppy The Persian's lead rope and began rummaging through the contents of the grooming box. He held up a blue and white can in the half-light and gave a triumphant smile.

'Bingo.'

'What is it?'

Cameron squinted as he read the label. 'Wow the Judges Touch Up. Covers stains, scars and blemishes. Does not wipe off, run or smear. Easily removed with an oil-based product such as our Wow the Judges High Gloss.' He stabbed the can with his index finger. 'It says sorrel. That's chestnut to you and me.'

Cameron bent over the grooming box again and pulled out another spray can. 'Wow the Judges High Gloss. Try that.'

Poppy hesitated. 'What if he freaks? Cloud hates the sound of aerosols.'

'I'd say he's probably used to it, wouldn't you?'

Cameron was right. Eddie Eaglestone must have been dyeing the stallion's blaze for years. Poppy gave the can a gentle shake and sprayed her handkerchief. The Persian didn't flinch. She rubbed again at the big stallion's forehead. This time when she held the cotton to the light, it was smeared with brown. Poppy pictured Micky Murphy's stained fingers. It hadn't been nicotine after all.

'Yesss!' cried Cameron. '*Now* we have proof.'

'I wouldn't be so sure,' said a voice smoothly behind them.

165

Poppy stifled a scream and the lead rope slipped through her fingers as a figure stepped out of the shadows. Startled, The Persian whipped around as quick as an eel and stood at the back of his box, his head high and his nostrils flared.

'Come come, Flight. It's only me,' Eddie Eaglestone purred.

'He's not Flight, he's The Persian. You stole him from my father!' Cameron cried.

'And what makes you think that?'

'Dad knew. He just couldn't prove it.'

'And exactly what yarn did the great Cormac O'Sullivan spin you?'

'He told me about the bidding war and how desperate you were to get your hands on The Persian. He was the best bred Arabian to come out of the Middle East and you wanted him for yourself. And then Dad outbid you by a couple of thousand pounds. You must have been furious.'

Eaglestone's fists were clenched like hand grenades by his sides. Poppy shrank backwards. What was Cameron thinking, goading him like this? The man was ruthless and dangerous, as unpredictable as a Pit Bull Terrier. Provoking him was like poking a stick into a nest of vipers. Who knew what he might do.

'You couldn't bear the fact that Dad had something you wanted, could you?' Cameron continued. Poppy gave him an imploring look. *Please don't*, she silently willed him. But the floodgates had opened and there was no stopping him. 'So you had our head groom beaten up, planted Micky Murphy at our yard and two weeks later he stole The Persian from under Dad's nose.'

Eaglestone gave a bark of laughter and Poppy felt the balance of power shift inside the barn. Cameron watched, wary as an alleycat, as the stud owner strode over to The Persian and ran his thumb over the smudged diamond on his forehead. When he turned back to look at them the anger on his face had been replaced by derision. Poppy wasn't sure which was worse.

'Your father never deserved to own a horse as great as this. Thanks to me Flight has helped secure the future of Arabian horses. His progeny are succeeding in all disciplines across Europe. They are the finest horses of their generation and they will go on to produce ever more perfect specimens of their breed. Your father would never have let him reach his full potential,' Eaglestone mocked. 'He wanted him for his own private petting zoo.'

'Dad loved The Persian for the horse he was, not for the glory and status he could give him,' said Cameron.

Eaglestone shrugged. 'Then he was a fool. This horse is the golden ticket, a licence to print money. And now your father is out of the way he is my pass to recognition in the Arab world.'

'You *were* waiting for Dad to die before you opened the stud to the public!'

Eaglestone was silent for a beat. Poppy held her breath.

'I couldn't take the risk that he would recognise Flight.'

Cameron stepped forward. A muscle twitched in his jaw. 'So you're admitting you did steal him?'

Poppy's hand closed around her mobile. What if he was about to come clean? If only she could record his confession, as she had when George Blackstone had admitted stealing Chester. It would be the evidence they needed for the police to charge him after all these years. But her phone was as dead as the proverbial dodo. She willed Cameron to look at her but his eyes were fixed on Eaglestone.

The older man exhaled impatiently. 'I didn't steal him. I don't get my hands dirty. I have Micky for that. He gave the grooms a dead cert tip on a race and they were at the pub getting drunk on their winnings when he pulled on his balaclava and led Flight straight past the CCTV cameras into a waiting horsebox.'

'Didn't the police question him at the time?' said Poppy.

Eaglestone shot her a contemptuous look. 'Of course they did. But he'd spent the early part of the evening with the others at the pub. By the time he slipped out they were all so legless they didn't even notice he'd gone. They were falling over themselves to give him a rock solid alibi.'

'What about the CCTV? The police must have looked at that,' Poppy persisted.

Eaglestone sneered. 'It was useless. The shots were so grainy they were about as much use as a chocolate teapot. It was a substandard CCTV system. Not like mine,' he boasted, gesturing at tiny cameras blinking red lights at them from all four corners of the barn. 'They're the best money can buy.'

'Fingerprints?' said Poppy, without much hope.

'Micky's prints were all over the place, but they would be - he worked there. And he stayed on for another couple of months so he didn't arouse suspicion. No-one ever suspected him of the theft.'

'Dad did,' said Cameron quietly. 'He always said there was something shifty about Micky Murphy, but no-one listened. No-one except me.'

'Perhaps he should have been more careful. It was all so easy. It's almost as though Cormac wanted the horse stolen. And he was insured, wasn't he? Your precious father probably welcomed the insurance money. I heard he'd spent his fortune on fast cars and not so fast horses by the end.'

'How dare you say that!' Cameron cried, squaring up to Eaglestone. But the older man batted him away with a dismissive wave of his hand.

'You're messing with things you should stay well out of. I thought you and your friends would get the message when I sent you across the river, but it seems I underestimated you.'

'That was you?' Poppy whispered. 'Flynn could have died.'

Cameron produced his phone from his back pocket and waved it in Eaglestone's face. 'I'm calling the police. I'm going to tell them everything.'

'And they're going to believe two kids over an upstanding member of the community like me?' he jeered. 'You're deluded, my son.'

'Don't you *dare* call me that!' Cameron hissed, lunging towards Eaglestone. The stud owner balled a fist and lashed out at him, connecting with his face with a crack that left Poppy light-headed with shock. Cameron cried out in surprise and crumpled to the ground clutching his jaw. His phone spun out of his hand and landed in the straw at Eaglestone's feet.

Unthinking, Poppy stepped forward. 'You can't do that!'

Eaglestone stood over her, his large frame blocking out the light from the window high above. He kicked the phone into the shadows.

'It's nothing more than he deserved. Perhaps he'll get the message now. And lucky for you I'm an old-fashioned sort and don't believe in hitting girls. So take your *friend*,' he spat, 'and clear off before I change my mind.'

He turned on his heels and stalked out of the barn. Poppy sank to her knees and gave Cameron's shoulder a gentle shake.

'You OK?'

Cameron nodded. His face was ghostly pale apart from a blemish the colour of wine on his left cheek.

'Call the police,' he muttered.

Poppy sank down on the straw next to him. 'I can't. Battery's flat, remember. And even if I could, he's right, isn't he? Who's going to believe us?'

Poppy was helping Cameron to his feet when the sound of raised voices outside the barn grew louder. She froze, the hairs on the back of her neck sending a warning signal to her legs, which turned to jelly and almost buckled under her.

'What if he's sent Micky Murphy to finish us off?' she whispered to Cameron.

He raised his eyebrows. 'It's Scarlett and Hannah. Can't you hear them bickering?'

Poppy cocked her head. He was right. She smiled in relief. Never had she been so glad to hear her two closest friends doing what they did best.

'I still say we should have tried the house first,' Hannah was grumbling.

'Are you mad? There's no way they'll still be there.' Scarlett was incredulous.

'So where the heck are they, clever clogs?'

'Here,' croaked Poppy. 'We're in here.'

The barn door swung open and the two girls charged in.

'Are you OK?' cried Scarlett, registering Poppy's pale face.

'Did you see Eaglestone?' Cameron demanded.

Scarlett shook her head.

'We tried to keep him talking as long as possible, but he strode off, muttering something about having to see a boy about a horse,' said Hannah.

'And then five minutes later we saw him race off down the drive in his Rolls Royce with Micky Murphy in the passenger seat,' said Scarlett.

Poppy and Cameron exchanged a glance.

'He knew you knew, didn't he? said Scarlett.

Cameron fingered his jaw and nodded. 'Can I use your phone?'

'There's no way they'll believe us,' said Poppy again.

They were huddled outside the barn waiting for the police to arrive.

'Looks like we're about to find out,' Hannah remarked, as a patrol car headed towards them.

The police car pulled up and two officers climbed out. When Poppy saw one was PC Claire Bodiam she almost wept with relief.

'Hello Poppy,' she said, her eyes crinkling at the corners. 'We mustn't keep meeting like this.'

Poppy blushed. She never set out to find trouble, but trouble always seemed to find her.

PC Bodiam patted her arm. 'You look like you've had a bit of a shock. You'd better tell us what this is all about.'

An hour later PC Bodiam closed her pocket notebook with a snap and eyed the four teenagers.

'So you're OK for a lift home?'

Poppy nodded. 'Caroline's coming to pick us up.'

'Righto. PC Bennett and I need to get back to the station but I'll be over later to take statements.'

'Thanks so much, PC Bodiam. For believing us I mean,' said Poppy in a small voice.

'My pleasure, Poppy.' The officer chuckled. 'And you might as well call me Claire. I reckon we must be on first name terms by now, don't you?'

They watched the tail lights of the police car grow smaller as it disappeared down the drive.

'D'you think they'll find them?' said Poppy.

'Of course they will,' said Scarlett. 'They have Automatic Number Plate Recognition and everything these days. I've seen it on *Police, Camera, Action!* And Eddie's golden Roller's not exactly an everyday sort of a car, is it?'

Poppy supposed her friend was right. 'But d'you think they have enough evidence to arrest them?'

'They've seized the can of dye and Claire took photos of The Persian and the red mark on Cameron's face. They seemed to take you seriously,' said Hannah.

She was right. Poppy hadn't been sure at first. Both officers had listened in silence as Cameron had turned the clock back eight years to the night The Persian had been stolen from the stables of a rock star far away across the Irish Sea. Poppy had thought she'd detected a look of disbelief on PC Bennett's face as they'd told how they'd suspected Eaglestone had passed the colt off as his own for all these years. But when they took the officers into the barn and showed them The Persian's diamond-shaped star, the can of Wow the Judges Touch Up and her own brown-stained handkerchief, any scepticism had been wiped off his face. And when Poppy had described how Eaglestone had lashed out at Cameron, PC Bennett had taken him out into the light and examined his jaw with gentle fingers.

'It doesn't look broken, but I advise you get it X-rayed as a precaution,' he'd said gruffly.

'Nah, you're alright, I'll be grand,' Cameron had grinned. 'And anyway, you should have seen the other guy.'

Charlie was, as Poppy could have predicted, absolutely gutted that he'd missed out on all the drama.

'So Eddie the Eaglestone may not be an Olympic ski jumper, but he is a real-life crime lord,' he said. 'Who'd have thought it?'

'I think crime lord might be pushing it, Charlie. He stole a horse, that's all,' said Poppy. She had decided not to tell Caroline and her dad about the false clue Eaglestone had set them that had so nearly ended in disaster. It wasn't worth raising their blood pressure.

'Not just any horse,' said Cameron.

'Not just any horse,' Poppy agreed.

'Who's looking after The Persian and the other horses tonight?' asked Caroline.

'The stud's other stablehands. Claire - that's PC Bodiam - said they had -' Poppy paused as she remembered the officer's exact words. 'Eliminated them from their enquiries.'

'So they reckon only Eaglestone and Murphy were in on it?' said Poppy's dad.

'So it seems,' said Cameron. He'd looked less brooding ever since the two police officers had driven away and there was a sparkle in his green eyes that hadn't been there before.

Freddie, curled in his bed by the range, lifted his black and tan head and woofed softly. Moments later there was a knock at the door.

'I'll go,' said Poppy, darting out of the kitchen.

She opened the door to PC Bodiam and her boss, the portly Inspector Bill Pearson.

'Have you found them?' she blurted.

Inspector Pearson was giving nothing away. 'Is Mr Walsh inside?'

Poppy held the door open and pointed down the hallway. 'In the kitchen.'

Caroline had already filled the kettle and was reaching in the cupboard for the biscuit tin. 'I've only got chocolate digestives. Is that OK?' she said as the inspector introduced himself to Cameron.

'That'll do nicely,' he said, winking at Charlie. The policeman's penchant for digestives was well-known. Caroline handed him a mug of tea and he dunked his biscuit in it and regarded them over steepled fingers with his seen-it-all policeman's eyes.

'Do you want the good news or the bad news?'

'The good news,' said Poppy, sitting on her chair with a thump.

'The good news is that Eaglestone and Murphy triggered ANPR and were pulled over by one of our traffic cars on the M5 just this side of Bristol. Eaglestone has been arrested on suspicion of assault. We looked at false imprisonment but decided it might be stretching it. He's also been arrested for conspiracy to steal. Murphy has been arrested for the theft of a horse. They are both in custody at Plymouth.'

Cameron and Charlie fist-bumped. Inspector Pearson cleared his throat.

'The bad news is that evidentially we are on sticky ground. I think we'll have enough to run with the assault charge, but as for stealing a horse eight years ago, I'm not so sure. Unless they admit it.'

'Which is unlikely, I would imagine,' said Poppy's dad.

'Highly unlikely,' said Inspector Pearson. 'So far they've both gone no comment. And Eaglestone's a slippery fish. Our Serious and Organised Crime Team have had their suspicions about him for years but have never been able to pin anything on him.'

'So if you were able to prove he'd stolen The Persian everyone'd be happy,' said Cameron.

Inspector Pearson took a large bite of biscuit, scattering crumbs over his belly. He flicked them off with a wave of his hand.

'They would,' he agreed.

'But he admitted it to us. Surely that counts?' cried Poppy.

PC Bodiam cradled her mug in her hands. 'It's his word against yours. And because it happened so long ago, the CPS might decide it's not in the public interest to charge them.'

'Who's the CPS?' said Charlie, his eyes like saucers.

'The Crown Prosecution Service. They're the ones who prosecute criminal cases. We just investigate them.'

Inspector Pearson helped himself to a second biscuit and dunked it into his tea. 'My opposite number in the Garda has sent over the original case file and I had a quick read before we came over. Apart from his white markings, the horse has no freeze marks and he wasn't microchipped. Unfortunately the vet who stitched his leg all those years ago had a fire at his surgery a couple of years later and all the records were destroyed. I had a look at the CCTV images too, and Eaglestone was right when he told you they were next to useless.'

'What about blood or DNA tests?' said Caroline suddenly. 'If you could prove The Persian and Fearless Flight were one and the same that would be enough for a prosecution, wouldn't it?'

'I'm right in thinking your father bought The Persian from the Middle East?' Inspector Pearson asked Cameron.

He nodded. 'His band was playing in Dubai. After the gig Dad was invited to look around an Arabian stud. He fell in love with this golden colt and when it was auctioned a couple of months later put in a sealed bid. My mum said he was choked when he heard The Persian was his.'

'I'm afraid we don't have the resources to test the horse's parents, even if we could track them down. And testing his progeny will prove nothing.'

Inspector Pearson stared glumly into his mug. Cameron ran a hand through his hair in frustration. But Poppy's mind was whirring. Something the inspector had said had triggered a memory. And it was the clue they were looking for, she was sure of it.

39

P oppy played the conversation back in her head.

'The CCTV!' she cried.

'Inspector Pearson said it was next to useless, Poppy,' said her dad gently.

'Not Cormac's CCTV. Eddie Eaglestone's CCTV! He told us his cameras were the best money could buy. And there were four of them in the barn. They would have filmed everything!'

The inspector glanced at PC Bodiam. 'Radio Control, Claire. See if we've still got anyone out at Eaglestone's place.'

The PC reached for her radio and disappeared into the hallway.

'I can see that would prove the assault, but it wouldn't prove his confession,' said Caroline.

'Ah, that's where you're wrong, Mrs McKeever. Some of these new-fangled CCTV systems record sound as well as pictures. We just have to hope Eddie Eaglestone was right when he said his was top of the range.'

Seven pairs of eyes swivelled around as PC Bodiam reappeared.

'Well?' said Inspector Pearson.

'Johnno's still there, guv. He's going to take a look.'

'So now we wait,' said the inspector.

Caroline offered him the plate of biscuits.

He smiled and took two. 'Thank you, Mrs McKeever. Don't mind if I do.'

THE WAIT WAS INTERMINABLE. PC Bodiam took Poppy's and Cameron's statements while Caroline and Hannah started preparing dinner and Inspector Pearson chatted to Poppy's dad about the weather. Charlie had found an old ring-bound notebook and was mimicking PC Bodiam as she scribbled the statements in her pocket notebook.

When PC Bodiam's mobile finally rang and they all jumped about a foot in the air Poppy realised she wasn't the only one on tenterhooks. The police officer held the phone to her ear and began pacing the length of the kitchen.

'Speaking. Uh huh. I see. Right. OK. Yes, he's with me now. I'll let him know. We'll see you back at the nick. Thanks Johnno.'

She ended the call. Poppy crossed her fingers.

'Looks like Poppy was onto something. Eaglestone's all singing, all dancing CCTV system does record sound. As we could narrow the timeframe to within a couple of minutes, Johnno's been able to find the footage from all four cameras in the barn and play it back. The first three recorded the pictures, so we've got the assault on film, but they were too far away to record the sound.'

Charlie groaned.

'And the fourth?' said Inspector Pearson.

PC Bodiam smiled. 'It was the one directly above The Persian's stall and it's recorded everything. It's all on there,

Guv, the whole confession. It's the proof we needed to secure a charge.'

The inspector slapped the table in satisfaction. 'Good work! Well-spotted, Poppy. We'll make a detective of you yet. And you, young Charlie-me-lad,' he added, standing and ruffling Charlie's hair.

Charlie beamed with pleasure. Poppy could have sworn he muttered, 'Thanks Guv,' under his breath.

'So what happens now?' said Cameron.

'We'll meet Johnno back at the nick and make sure CID have the footage and your statements before they next question Eaglestone and Murphy. We need to liaise with the Garda, because strictly speaking the theft is their case, but with any luck we'll have them charged by the morning and before the courts in the next couple of days,' said Inspector Pearson.

'What'll happen to The Persian?' said Hannah.

'Did Cormac leave a will?' said Inspector Pearson.

Cameron nodded. 'He left everything - well, what's left of everything - to me and Mum.'

'So he'll be yours. You might have to wait until court proceedings are over, but the horse'll be taken to an approved yard and looked after until then.'

Cameron nodded again and gazed out of the kitchen window. It seemed to Poppy that he was trying to collect himself.

'Thank you,' he said finally. 'That's grand.'

40

Poppy woke the next morning to the sound of purring. She prised open her eyes to see Magpie staring at her owlishly a few centimetres from her face.

'Too early,' Poppy mumbled. But the old cat was not to be deterred and began kneading her shoulder with razor sharp claws.

'Ow, that hurts,' Poppy told him. She checked her alarm clock. Ten to six. Far too early. Sighing, she wriggled upright and scooped Magpie onto her lap. He circled three times, curled himself into a ball and promptly fell asleep.

Poppy glanced down at the tangle of duvet on Hannah's camp bed.

'Hey Han, you awake?' she whispered.

When there was no answer Poppy gently eased Magpie off her lap and pulled back Hannah's duvet. The camp bed was empty. Poppy peered through the curtains. A low mist clung to the ground like dry ice at a pop concert, but the sky was a hazy blue, promising a warm day ahead.

Cloud was grazing in the far corner of the paddock, flanked by a donkey on either side. Hannah, wearing pyjamas and wellies, was leaning against the gate watching them. Poppy found a fleece in the pile of clothes on the floor by her bed and ran down to join her.

'Hey,' said Hannah with a wan smile.

'Hey,' said Poppy. 'Everything OK?'

'Yes.' Hannah rested her chin on her hands. 'I couldn't sleep.'

'Neither could Magpie,' said Poppy with a wry smile. 'What time's your dad due?'

'About eleven. He wanted to miss the worst of the traffic.'

Poppy leant on the gate and they watched Cloud, Chester and Jenny in companionable silence.

'I'm going to miss all this,' Hannah said eventually, waving her hands at the fields and the dark purple shadow of the Riverdale tor beyond. 'It's been a blast.'

'It has,' agreed Poppy. 'But you'll be back, won't you? And we'll still be here.'

Hannah nodded. 'I wonder if Cameron's home yet.'

Poppy's dad had driven him to Exeter Airport the previous evening. He'd been due to land in Dublin at half past eight.

'I should think so. He seemed a lot happier, didn't he? Like a weight had been lifted off his shoulders.'

Cameron had hoisted his rucksack onto his back as if it weighed less than a feather and down pillow and had shaken their hands one by one. When he reached Poppy he had clasped her fingers tightly and said, 'Thank you for helping me find my golden horse.'

Poppy had smiled back. 'It was my pleasure.'

'He did,' Hannah agreed. 'Unlike Georgia La-di-da Canning.'

Poppy stifled a snort of laughter. Once Inspector Pearson and PC Claire Bodiam had left she had texted Georgia. She'd wanted to apologise for blaming her for fixing the clues. Georgia, to give her credit, had texted straight back.

No worries. I can see why you thought it was me. Believe me, I'd have blamed you if the boot had been on the other foot.

Poppy had been glad the older girl had accepted her apology with good grace. Although they would never be close friends she respected Georgia's ruthless ambition and admired her total disregard for other people's opinions. In fact sometimes she wished she could be a little more Georgia, a little less Poppy. And she knew that Georgia's life at Claydon Manor was not the rose-tinted paradise Scarlett seemed to think it was.

Poppy's phone had pinged again. A grin had spread across her face as she'd read a second text from Georgia.

And BTW Eddie Eaglestone is a complete and utter shyster. My uncle used to be a jeweller and checked out the 'golden horse'. It's actually copper. Go figure.

Poppy's fingers had tapped back a reply.

Looks like we were all taken in. But don't worry - Mr Eaglestone is about to get his comeuppance. I'll dish the dirt next time we go for a hack. Spk soon x

'It was all smoke and mirrors,' said Poppy now. 'Eddie Eaglestone's empire was built on a lie. Inspector Pearson told Caroline the force's financial investigators are going to start digging into his business empire. They've always thought his casinos were used to launder dirty money apparently. Looks like stealing The Persian was the tip of the iceberg.'

Cloud wandered over and Poppy scratched his ear absentmindedly.

Hannah gave a loud sigh.

'What's up?' said Poppy.

'No-one back home's going to believe a word of this, you know. They'll think all the country air has gone to my head.'

Poppy laughed. 'You ought to stick around, kid. There's never a dull moment at Riverdale, is there Cloud? Adventures are what we do best.'

AFTERWORD

Thank you for reading *The Hunt for the Golden Horse*. If you enjoyed this book it would be great if you could spare a couple of minutes to write a quick review on Amazon. I'd love to hear your feedback!

ABOUT THE AUTHOR

Amanda Wills is the Amazon bestselling author of The Riverdale Pony Stories, which follow the adventures of pony-mad Poppy McKeever and her beloved Connemara Cloud.

She is also the author of the Mill Farm Stables series of pony books and Flick Henderson and the Deadly Game, a fast-paced mystery about a super-cool new heroine who has her sights set on becoming an investigative journalist.

Amanda, a UK-based former journalist who now works part-time as a police press officer, lives in Kent with her husband and fellow indie author Adrian Wills and their sons Oliver and Thomas.

Find out more at www.amandawills.co.uk or at www.-facebook.com/riverdaleseries or follow amandawillsauthor on Instagram.

www.amandawills.co.uk
amanda@amandawills.co.uk

Printed by Amazon Italia Logistica S.r.l.
Torrazza Piemonte (TO), Italy

16527428R00114